# A Broken Heart Mended

## Crooked Arrow Ranch, Book 1

### Jenna Hendricks

# Contents

# *Books by Jenna Hendricks*

**Triple J Ranch –**
Book 0 - Finding Love in Montana (Join my newsletter to get this book for free)

Book 1 - Second Chance Ranch – also available on audio

Book 2 – Cowboy Ranch – also available on audio

Book 3 – Runaway Cowgirl Bride

Book 4 – Faith of A Cowboy

Book 5 – Cowboy Blessings

Book 6 – The Cowboy's Game

**Big Sky Christmas –**

Book 1 – Her Montana Christmas Cowboy

Book 2 – Her Christmas Rodeo Cowboy

Book 3 – Her Mistletoe Cowboy

Book 4 – Her Sleigh Ride Christmas Cowboy

**Crooked Arrow Ranch-**

Book 1 – A Broken Heart Mended

Book 2 – Hope's Healing Love

Book 3 – Love's Healing Balm

**Standalone books –**

Christmas Crazy In July

# Newsletter Sign-up

B y signing up for my newsletter, you will get a free copy of the prequel to the Triple J Ranch series, Finding Love in Montana. As well as another free book from J.L. Hendricks.

And for a limited time, the prequel to the new Crooked Arrow Ranch series, Wounded Hearts, will also be included.

If you want to make sure you hear about the latest and greatest, sign up for my newsletter at: Subscribe to Jenna Hendricks' newsletter. I will only send out a few e-mails a month. I'll do cover reveals, snippets of new books, and giveaways or promos in the newsletter, some of which will only be available to newsletter subscribers.

*Chapter 1*

Nelly Wilson parked her Chevy truck outside the Frenchtown Roasting Company and sighed when she took in the scents of coffee and sweetness. She'd just driven twelve hours that day, after three other long days of driving from Georgia to get there in time to have the weekend to settle in, and she was exhausted and hungry. A black coffee and cinnamon roll were exactly what she needed and deserved.

When she exited her truck, the four dogs in the back began to bark and whimper.

"Nein, halt." Nelly reached into the dog crate closest to her. The dogs had done so well with their travel, but even they were getting tired of the drive. "Braver hund." She rubbed between Rogue's ears, and he settled down again. She couldn't ignore the rest of her pack. So she moved around the truck bed and scratched or rubbed each dog and spoke to them in their German commands, calling them good dogs—"Braver hund."

Even though she did speak to them in English a lot, she also tried to reinforce their German command training. She'd already successfully placed six different dogs with patients who were doing very well with their service dogs. And these four were on their way to being even better than the rest.

"I promise, once I have my coffee and bun, I'll take you all for a walk before we find our new home." She grinned at her dogs, knowing that while they didn't fully understand what she was saying, they did know she'd take exceptional care of them.

She could only pray that the coffee shop was still open. It was just past six at night, and in small towns the coffee shops usually closed after lunch. When she walked up to the door and noticed the sign still read *open*, she breathed a sigh of relief. "Thank you, Lord."

But when she turned the door handle, it wouldn't budge.

Nelly pounded on the door and looked through the window. "Oh, come on. I need the caffeine and sugar."

A barista was behind the counter, and from Nelly's angle it looked like she was counting her till. Nelly looked for a sign stating their hours. It was Friday night and the sign said they were open until nine, so why was the door locked and the cashier counting out?

"Please, I just need a black coffee and I'll take any pastry you have. I can pay in cash," Nelly yelled through the window when the barista looked up at her.

The woman bit her upper lip and looked around. Then she put the cash drawer back in the till and walked to the front door. When she unlocked and opened the door, Nelly smiled and profusely thanked the girl.

"I'll leave a good tip, I swear. I just need coffee and sugar. I'll take whatever you have. Even if the coffee is only warm, I'll be happy with it. I promise." Nelly held up her hand as though she was being sworn in at a hearing.

"I don't know. I was supposed to close early tonight. The head barista is getting married tomorrow and I'm supposed to join them for the rehearsal dinner tonight." The barista looked back over her shoulder at the pastry counter. "All I have left is one cinnamon roll. The coffee is still hot, but I've already cleaned the espresso machines, so I can't make anything fancy."

Nelly waved her hands and grinned. "That's perfect. I'm not into froufrou coffee. I like mine strong and black." An image of her ex passed through her mind, and she tried so hard to block it out. He used to always tease her that the only reason she liked her coffee strong and black was because that was how she liked her men. She didn't always date black men. In fact, she never really paid much attention to the color of a person's skin. When she really thought about it, she'd probably dated men from a variety of races. All she cared about was what was on the inside, and if they loved the Lord. She only dated Christians.

Skin color didn't make the man, it was the heart that made the difference between a good man and a scallywag.

"And a cinnamon roll is my favorite. Can you heat it up?" Nelly looked hopeful as the barista opened the door and let her inside.

Instead of eating in the shop, she respected the girl's need to get going. The tag on her shirt read Anise. And Nelly didn't want to keep Anise from joining her boss at the rehearsal dinner.

"Thank you, Anise! I'll be back for more coffee and treats this weekend. Have fun tonight." As she left, Nelly was sure to put a generous tip in the jar. And when she got back in her truck, that was when she noticed the handwritten sign stating the shop was closing early for the rehearsal of Dana and Jerod.

A twinge of regret entered Nelly's heart. She would have already married Mick if she'd not decided to completely change her life. It didn't do to dwell on the past, and she knew it. It was time to look forward.

Nelly's forward momentum took her to her new home as she left her past where it belonged.

"Alright, kiddos. We're home," Nelly announced when she pulled up in front of her new ranch-style home that also sported a large barn in the back. From the pictures she had seen, it would be perfect for the dogs to kennel in.

The outside wasn't exactly what she expected. Sure, there was a wraparound porch, but it needed to be scraped and several coats of paint would make it look new again. One of the windows had been broken and boarded up. "Hm, well. Maybe the inside is better than the outside?" She looked down at her dogs and shrugged.

But when she opened the front door of the house, her mouth dropped open and she almost cried.

The dogs did it for her. It was their whines and whimpers that brought Nelly out of the momentary stupor that had claimed her mind.

"How in the world? This is nothing like the photos the Realtor showed me." The smell hit her before her foot crossed the threshold.

Even Rogue, who was fantastic at making his own disgusting smells, whined and backed out of the house, almost hitting Nelly's leg.

"Why, that good for nothing...weasel! How could he show me pictures that had to be years old?" Knowing it was her fault for not coming to see it in person, but not actually wanting to admit it, she backed out of the pig sty and covered her mouth.

"No, that's not right. Calling this place a pig sty is an assault on all pigs. Something, or several somethings, must have died here." She sat down hard on the porch steps and yelped when a board below her cracked. "Now what?"

Nelly jumped up and walked away from the house. A real fear of the place crashing down around her filled her heart.

Buffy, a chocolate retriever and her only female dog, rubbed up against her leg in support. Instinctively, Nelly reached down to pet the wonderful dog who was lending her support and warmth. Not that it was cold outside, just a figurative warmth that was missing from this place.

On her other side, Spike, a male golden retriever, scootched closer to her. "You guys, and gal, are the best. Thank you. Braver hund." She patted their heads.

A distant bark caught her attention and she looked around. "Buffy, Spike, Angel. Okay, Rogue is that you?" Nelly took off around the house to see if she could find the source of the barking. All three of the other dogs were at her heels, tongues lolling with the excitement.

The sight was not what she expected. Yes, Rogue was standing there, almost pointing like a pointer who'd spotted a duck. But instead of a dead duck on the ground waiting for her to pick up and put in the pack for supper, she found something much more to her liking, and the dogs—if their wagging tails were any indicator—appreciated it as well.

A large red barn with white trim looked to be in almost pristine shape. Quite a dichotomy from the view of the ranch house. The keychain the Realtor sent her had several keys on it, and she hoped one of them was to the barn. If the outside was any indication, then at least the dogs would have a safe, dry place to sleep that night. And maybe, just maybe, if the good Lord was looking out for her, she'd have a safe place to rest her head for the night as well.

"Well, the doors won't open themselves." Nelly looked down to her four dogs sitting on their haunches just waiting for her to do something. She put her hand out, palm down and commanded, "Bleib." She tried to keep her commands in German as much as possible, even when they weren't technically working. It was simpler for the dogs and would keep them from misunderstanding.

Nelly took the keys she still held in her left hand and proceeded to open the barn door. With a sharp intake of breath, she about had a heart attack. "Whoa. Not what I was expecting. Not at all."

Rogue growled behind her, and she listened to his warning. While she didn't feel a threat, she did sense something weird going on in the barn. Without turning her head, she motioned for them to follow. "Heir."

In almost unison, with Rogue taking the lead, all four took up positions on her flank.

"Hello? Is anyone in here?" Even though she felt the place was deserted, Nelly wanted to give anyone a chance to come forward. If they surprised the dogs, they might not like what happened.

While all four dogs were trained very well, they were also extremely protective of Nelly. They would feel her trepidation and most likely they'd feel the same way. Especially if a man came from nowhere.

Slowly, she took a few steps and looked around in awe.

If the house had been taken over by animals, this place was surely saved from anything, or anyone. In fact, it looked like someone had been keeping it up quite nicely for some time. The interior was sparkling clean, for a barn. Fresh straw lay on the ground, and each horse stall had a door on it that provided a bit of privacy for the animal.

There were no animals present, other than her dogs. That much she was sure of. Her dogs would have at least whined if another animal was present that they hadn't been introduced to. Nelly watched her dogs. They sniffed the air but didn't seem the least bit upset. Other than the growl that emanated from Rogue when she opened the door, they didn't seem to be the least bit worried.

"Rogue, Lauf." Nelly pointed forward, indicating the direction she wanted the dog to check. The other three dogs stood there waiting for their directions, and when she pointed where each one was to go, they went quietly and without any issue.

Nelly couldn't have been prouder if they were her own kids. All four searched their areas without a peep. When they were done, they came back and dutifully sat on their haunches next to her.

"Well, I guess that means we're safe." She took a few more steps inside and peered into the horse stalls closest to the barn door. While the sun was in the process of setting outside, there was very little light inside.

Even though it was early June, this was Montana and the sun set close to nine at night, which meant she needed to hurry up and find the light switch. Before she left Atlanta, Nelly had arranged for the power to be turned on at the property. It wasn't big, just enough space for her dogs to train. But she would need power and water to get started.

Nelly noticed a large propane tank on the side of the barn. She made a mental note to check it tomorrow to make sure she had enough fuel to power whatever ran off propane. Probably a gas stove, water heater, house heater, and maybe even some lights.

It didn't take long to find the switch; it was located to the right of the barn door. With the flip switched up, she could see even more of the immaculate barn. If she didn't know any better, she'd think an entire cleaning crew had come through the day before and spruced the place up for her.

As she began a slow inspection of the place, she noticed a set of stairs in the back. When she crested the top of the stairs, she praised God for providing. On the other side of the locked door was a bed. It was only a twin bed, but the mattress looked to be in good shape. She had a box of linens she could make work, at least long enough to figure out what she was going to do for sleeping arrangements while she fixed the house.

There was no way on God's green earth she was going to sleep in that cesspool of garbage and animal carcasses. "How is it possible this place is so pristine while the house should be bulldozed?" Nelly shook her head.

She unloaded her truck into the barn and got the dogs settled for the night before she went upstairs with a hot cup of peppermint tea. In her search, she also located a breakroom of sorts that had an electric tea kettle and running water in the sink.

Her last thought before drifting off into a dreamless night of sleep was how good God was.

## *Chapter 2*

"**W**hat in tarnation is going on with all these blasted couples?" Sam Marley grumbled under his breath as he looked outside the barn door.

In the paddock, or the area that had once been a formal paddock but now was more like a staging area for whatever was going on at the time, a plethora of women and men stood dressed in their Sunday finest. But it wasn't Sunday afternoon—it was a Friday afternoon in May.

Sam had just come in from a long ride on Jackson, one of the only things he enjoyed these days. Horse riding calmed him like nothing else could. But that wasn't too surprising, since he'd come back from a war zone with more than physical scars to show his service. Service to a county that didn't seem to care about its returning heroes anymore.

"Sam! Hey, Sam!" Dana waved at him from the paddock in her white dress. She was so beautiful and sweet, and one of the nicest women he'd ever met. Jerod was one lucky son of a gun.

He tried to smile for her, but he just couldn't muster up the energy to move his lips. Instead, he walked outside to her beckoning call, hoping he didn't have a scowl on his face but knowing it was there just the same. Sam could never say no to Dana. Not when she had done so much to help the ranch and its owner.

Currently, Sam lived and worked on the Crooked Arrow Ranch just outside of Frenchtown, Montana. It was a one-light kinda town nestled along the main highway and along the lower edge of the snowcapped Rocky Mountains. On a clear day they had a sweet view of the Great Plains, if one knew where to go. If he could choose anywhere to live, it would be here. At least the residents still supported and loved their military.

When Sam first joined the Army, his hometown had sent him off with a ticker tape parade. Well, okay, it wasn't exactly a ticker tape parade in his honor. And he did leave on July fifth, so maybe the town's Fourth of July parade wasn't exactly for him, but he was honored to ride with the major in his convertible car. It was the sweetest ride he'd ever been in.

Somehow the mayor of his small town of Bensford, South Dakota had acquired a rare and beautifully restored 1960 Cadillac Eldorado Biarritz Convertible Air. It had the sweetest rear fenders with the fins that had brake lights in them. The custom paint job was a cherry red with a high gloss. The interior was all black leather, the soft kind that felt good to sit in. Nothing at all like the pleather chairs in the diner that made embarrassing sounds when you scooted across the seat.

Sam grumbled under his breath that right now, no one loved him or the fact that he served. Which wasn't really true, but he wanted to feel sorry for himself since he was the only single guy in attendance that day. Even Mike, the quiet guy who preferred milking cows to talking to anyone—let alone a pretty gal—had a date for the big event.

Although, to be fair, Sam had never even tried to get himself a date. Why would he? A woman would take one look at him and run off screaming and waving her hands as though he was the beast trying to force her to stay with him and break his curse. Only, his life wasn't a fairy tale. He was a horribly scarred beast. No kiss from a pretty princess or the love of a local town girl would break a witch's curse.

His was a curse of war. The sort of curse that would stay with him until the day he died. The doctors had put him back together as though he was Humpty Dumpty, but it wasn't enough. He had missing parts. Parts that had been replaced by metal and plastic.

And don't even get Sam started on his mind.

"Sam, come on. We need you." Dana took two steps toward the grumpy, unhappy man. "Why aren't you dressed yet? The practice is going to start in less than ten minutes."

"Honey, he's fine. Let him do the practice in his Wranglers. It's no problem." Jerod nodded at Sam. "But tomorrow you'll be in your suit, right?"

"Why do I have to wear a monkey suit? It's not like I'm the one getting hitched." Sam looked down at his boots and muttered under his breath, "I'm never getting married."

"Sam Marley!" Dana Baker, soon to be Dana Stevens, pursed her lips and put fisted hands on her hips. "I don't want any negativity this weekend. You will put on a happy face."

Sam grumbled something incoherent.

With a sigh, Dana relaxed her pose. "Sam, aren't you happy for Jerod and me?"

Sam's head jerked up. "Of course I am."

"Then can you show it? Just a little bit?" Dana quirked her lips and looked at Sam. Not with pity, but hope. She had always believed Sam could turn his life around if only he had a better attitude.

Megan Anderson, the ranch's counselor, sauntered up in her flowery sundress and brown boots. She smiled from ear to ear. She was another one of those who'd recently gotten engaged and oozed love and happiness. "Sam, come on. Daniel's running late again." She looked to Dana and rolled her eyes. "Why don't you walk me down the aisle in his place?"

Megan and Daniel were only one of the couples in the wedding party. Megan was a bridesmaid and Daniel was the groomsman lucky enough to walk her down the aisle. Soon, they'd be the bride and groom at their own wedding.

Daniel was the foreman at the local Christmas tree farm that had recently decided to expand into all seasons. They even had a plot of land devoted to spring and summer flowers. They were getting ready to have their first annual flower festival. And of course, the entire town supported their efforts.

Sam rolled his eyes. "Of course he is. He's got a farm to run. Why can't anyone understand when a man needs to work?" But he acquiesced and took Megan's arm in his. "Where do we stand?"

The wedding run-through went smoothly, and when Daniel finally showed up it was to take his spot with the groomsmen so Sam could go and sit down. Sam's job the day of the wedding was as an usher, which was why he hadn't dressed up for the rehearsal—there had been no need.

The fact that Megan had taken hold of his prosthetic left arm hadn't registered until he watched the couple walking back down the makeshift aisle. The wedding would be in the paddock area instead of a church. Then the reception would follow out on the grassy area where Jerod had put up a couple of large white tents.

The fact that he had forgotten about his missing arm for an hour wouldn't really hit him until later, after the dinner.

Instead, he paid attention to the disgustingly sweet couple of the night, Dana and Jerod. Although, Sam couldn't begrudge Jerod his happiness. Not after all he'd been through and everything Jerod was doing to help all those at the ranch.

"Honey, I can't wait until tomorrow afternoon when you'll officially be my wife." Jerod leaned down and kissed the tip of Dana's nose.

The action almost made Sam puke. "How can two people be so disgustingly sweet?"

Mike, who sat next to him at the dinner, laughed. "Sam"—he put a hand on Sam's shoulder

—"get used to it. The newlyweds will be living here at the ranch, and I'd bet big money we'll see much more than a quick peck on the nose."

"It's s'posed to be a place for us to heal, not get sicker." Sam grumbled and took a bite of the steak. Cutting steak wasn't easy for a man with a prosthetic left hand, but Megan had worked with him over the past few months and he was finally figuring out how to get the fake hand and fingers to work for him.

The rest of the evening, Sam did his best to ignore the happy couple, to no avail.

The Crooked Arrow Ranch was a place where injured servicemembers could go when the military doctors had done all they could to sew their pieces back together. Some days Sam felt more like a Raggedy Andy doll than a human. He also knew he looked like the doll made of rags. Then he'd remind himself that he did come home —alive. He may not be whole, but he wasn't sitting somewhere in a pine box with his momma crying over his flag. So that was good.

In addition to the physically injured coming to the ranch to heal and readjust to civilian life, those whose scars weren't physical also came to heal. Sam turned to see Mike Blankenship, one of the guys who'd been diagnosed with PTSD, smiling at the happy couple. Mike rarely smiled, but for some reason the man was happy tonight.

Should Sam be happy, too? He supposed he should. Dana had really helped Jerod get through the final vestiges of his PTSD. Since Dana had come along, Jerod was happy. Shoot, the man was practically glowing like a teenage boy taking the prettiest girl to prom. Which was sorta what was happening. Dana was one of the prettiest cowgirls in town. If he hadn't been such a curmudgeonly ol' coot—Dana's words, not his—then maybe he'd have had a chance with the pretty barista when he met her.

Nah, Sam wouldn't have had a chance. And he didn't want one. Still didn't, not with the other pain he still harbored. No, women weren't for him. Oh, he liked the fairer sex, no doubt about it. But they didn't like men who weren't whole. And Sam would never be a whole man. That was the real problem. Even with the fake arm the VA doctors set him up with, he wasn't all there—mentally or physically.

And as his ex had told him, who would want only part of a man?

Thoughts of the Fourth of July parade sending him off reentered his mind, and it gave him a stomachache.

Sam remembered riding in the mayor's car and waving at everyone as he passed by. The memory of one lady in particular jolted him. "Sam! I'll wait for you, I promise." Annabelle blew him a kiss that was only a sample of what had come later that night. She must have kissed him for hours before they were interrupted by her dad.

"Son, I know you're leaving tomorrow to serve our great nation, but sitting out here in your car kissing my daughter for hours on end isn't appropriate. When you're ready to talk about marriage, I'll be ready to listen. But until then, keep it wholesome and respect my daughter." Annabelle's dad didn't exactly scare Sam, but he sure did have the stature of someone he didn't want to mess with.

"Yes, sir. I'm sorry. I should have known better." Sam ducked his eyes and looked at the disheveled girl in the front seat of his car. His heart had always pitter-pattered when he thought of that moment.

It was the memory that kept him going when he was stuck in the sandpit.

It was the memory that came to him when he lay there on the side of a road after a roadside bomb took out his Humvee.

It was the memory that forced him to stay alive. He wasn't going to let her down, or break her heart by dying.

He mentally shook himself. The doctors told him to stop thinking about the past as it would do no good. Instead, he would work at learning how to use his left arm, or what there was of it, and then move on. Maybe he'd get a job on a ranch somewhere nearby, or maybe down in South America somewhere. Not speaking Spanish might make it simpler for him; he could focus on work and nothing else.

Until then, he'd have to deal with all these new couples.

Shoot, instead of Crooked Arrow Ranch, it should be renamed the Bachelor Ranch. Or Love Connection Ranch. Sam knew it wouldn't be much longer before all his compatriots were either married or engaged.

The feeling of being left behind filled his heart, and he wished, not for the first time, that he hadn't come home at all.

*Chapter 3*

Nelly's thoughts weren't exactly the same when she woke to her dogs barking the next morning. While she had trained them to sleep until seven in the morning, she had never bothered to train them to stay quiet once they woke. If only...

Her head ached as she got up and realized she should have eaten something more substantial than a cinnamon roll and cup of coffee for dinner. "Of all the nights to be bad and not eat something healthy," she grumbled.

Nelly sat on the edge of the bed and ran a hand down her face. She'd need to find a place to shower and a way to get a fridge and stove put in the barn, but until then she'd have to make do with what she had.

When she stood up, she stretched her achy muscles and yawned. "A new day, a new dawn." Her older brother used to say that every morning in high school. The sweet memory left a smile on her lips as she changed into work clothes and headed downstairs to release the hounds, so to speak.

"Guten Morgen." Nelly looked at the dogs sitting on the other side of the door of one stall. Usually she separated them for the night, but with everything going on she'd decided to let them all sleep together in one horse stall.

Today she'd get their kennels inside and set them up so the dogs could continue their ritual. It was important for their training that they had a sense of normalcy, even when moving. So as they went about their morning business in the fenced-in paddock next to the barn, she went to work getting a cup of morning tea. Once they were ready, she brought them in and set them up in their own stalls with some fresh water in their bowls as well as kibble in their food bowls.

Once the dogs were finished, she took them all with her back into town. First up was breakfast for her. Then off to see the no-good, swindling Realtor.

The moment she parked her truck outside the Frenchtown Roasting Company, the tension dripped from her shoulders and she took in the wonderful aroma of coffee brewing mixed with sugary goodness. "Hmm, cinnamon rolls." Even though it wasn't good to have cinnamon rolls for dinner, she was probably going to have them for breakfast today. She just needed to get going, that was all.

Nelly promised herself she'd have a good lunch and dinner.

Not expecting lines, or even a lot of people, she walked into the coffee shop with a smile on her face and expectations of sipping the hot goodness in only a few moments.

She stopped short just inside the door and her mouth gaped. The place was jam-packed with people of all races and ages talking and eating. There were two lines—one at the register to place to-go orders and one for getting a seat at the small grouping of tables in the center of the room. Nelly had thought she'd sit and eat, but now she changed her mind and headed straight to the takeout line.

While she waited, she eavesdropped on other conversations, which wasn't difficult to do considering how tightly packed they were in the room, and how loud everyone was.

A couple behind her was gushing over the tulips they had just seen as they drove from their hotel to the coffee shop. "Do you think the flowers at Big Sky Christmas Tree Farm will be as nice?"

The man with the woman grinned and put an arm around her shoulders. "Tina, I bet we'll see so much more than just a small amount of tulips. I expect we'll see the crocus flowers. And if we're lucky, we'll get the snakeskin one. What was that called again?"

They spoke about other flowers they hoped to see, but Nelly tuned them out. She liked flowers and would probably check out the flower displays, but it wasn't the foremost thought on her brain. At this point she needed coffee and sugar in that order, and lots and lots of it. Maybe she'd see if she could dive into a vat of coffee followed by a rinse in a pool of cinnamon-swirl icing.

Two cowboys standing in front of her caught her attention when they mentioned the wedding later that day.

"Say, why didn't Sam get a date for tonight?" the cowboy in the black hat asked the man in a red baseball cap.

Red-baseball-cap guy laughed. "Mike, get real. You know Sam's never gonna ask a woman out. And if he did, she'd probably die from shock."

Nelly furrowed her brow and prayed they weren't making fun of a man who had difficulty asking women out. Some men just needed a little nudge to feel confident. Not all of them felt confident enough to ask out a pretty girl. She cleared her throat when she felt herself getting ready to interrupt.

The sound caught their attention and both men turned.

The man in the red cowboy had looked at her face and grinned. "Why, howdy." He put his hand out. "I'm Skeeter. This here"—he pointed to his friend—"is Mike. Are you new to town?"

She shook his hand and appreciated that he held hers firmly, instead of like a limp noodle. So many men thought women couldn't give a proper shake.

Nelly grinned and introduced herself. "Yes, I just moved in last night."

Skeeter's eyes sparkled and he took a half step closer. "Really? Are you living in town?"

She shook her head. "Nope, I just bought the old Brown ranch. Or what's left of it." The Realtor had told her that most of the land had been split and sold to neighbors who wanted to expand their ranches, or fields. Nelly didn't want that much land, so she was happy to have the ten acres and no more.

Mike's eyes popped open and he gaped at her. "You're brave. Did you sleep inside the house?"

Skeeter grinned and looked her up and down. "Looks like you survived quite nicely."

The last thing Nelly needed was a man flirting with her. And from the looks of the guy, he was a few years her junior. She wasn't interested in playing the cougar to his cub. Instead of rolling her eyes like she wanted to, she pointed to the open space in front of the guys. "Looks like the line is moving forward."

Mike turned his head to look and his cheeks turned pink. "Sorry." He moved forward, leaving his buddy behind.

Skeeter only moved forward when she did. "So, is the house really as bad as everyone says?"

"Uh." Nelly rubbed the back of her neck. If the entire town knew how bad the place was, then they must have known what a scoundrel the Realtor was, right? "What do you know about Lank Rosenthal?"

Mike chuckled but didn't turn around. Instead, he stepped forward again as the line moved closer to the register.

"Lank?" Skeeter guffawed and slapped his hand on his thigh. "That scoundrel. I bet he didn't tell you how bad the place was, did he?"

"You got that right. At least the barn was in pristine shape. That's where I'll be bunking up until I can get the house in order." Nelly was starting to like these guys. Skeeter was a flirt, no doubt, but they seemed harmless. Or at least, her inner warning bells weren't ringing.

Mike turned around. "If you need help, reach out to Jerod at the Crooked Arrow Ranch. He can find some men who have the skills to help."

Skeeter shook his head. "Nah, not this week. He's getting hitched tonight and will be on his honeymoon all week."

"Oh, yeah." Mike turned his head down and looked forward again.

"But, if you want some muscle"—Skeeter flexed his arm to show off his bicep and grinned—"I'm your man."

"Stop bugging the poor woman and let her order her coffee," a gruff voice called out behind them.

Skeeter leaned back and looked around Nelly. "Ah, Sam. Not all humans disdain a morning conversation." He arched a brow and stood tall again, ignoring the glare he received from Sam.

Instead of agreeing with Skeeter, even though she did usually need coffee to get going, Nelly turned around to greet the man behind her. "Hi, I'm Nelly." She gave him a little wave.

Sam nodded and grunted, "I'm Sam. And if you need help his week, I can get a crew together on Monday. Like Skeeter said, Jerod will be out on his honeymoon all week."

Unsure who these men were, Nelly furrowed her brow. She would have asked what was going on, but Sam seemed to sense her confusion.

"I take it you don't know who we are?" She was struck by how stoic Sam seemed.

Nelly shook her head. "I'm sorry, but I just got in last night and am confused."

Sam scowled at Skeeter, then turned soft eyes to Nelly. "I'm sorry, my ranch hands can get ahead of themselves."

"*Your* ranch hands? Since when did you buy a stake in the Crooked Arrow?" For the first time since Nelly had met him, Skeeter frowned.

When Sam grinned, his face lit up. Nelly noticed his dark, curly hair that matched his soft brown eyes. The skin around his eyes crinkled when he smiled, giving her the only real sense of his age. The full beard he wore covered most of his face and hid any signs of age. She guessed he was in his mid- to late-thirties, but couldn't be sure. The sparkle in his eyes caught her breath, and she had to look away.

"If you recall, Jerod put me in charge of assignments while he's away." Sam crossed his arms over his chest. His biceps were thick and impressive, but one of his arms seemed thinner than the other.

Nelly looked a bit too long at his arms, and she noticed storm clouds had covered his face. He also put his left arm behind his back. Not sure what she had done to upset him, Nelly looked over his shoulder and noted the long line of patrons that now went out the door.

"Can I buy you a cup of coffee so we can discuss what it is your ranch does to help fix broken houses?" It was the least she could do since she had obviously upset him. Maybe he was the type who didn't like it when women checked him out? It was possible he was married. She didn't have time to check for a wedding band.

"I can buy my own coffee." Sam's gruff voice sent her stumbling back into Skeeter.

Hands went up to stop her from moving farther into a hard chest. "Don't pay him no mind, he's just a curmudgeonly ol' coot. I'd be happy to discuss your housing needs and I'll buy you a coffee."

Nelly turned to see Skeeter, a nice-looking man with a huge smile. His open and friendly nature pulled her in. "Thanks, but I also need breakfast. I would, however, be interested in learning more about the Crooked Arrow Ranch. I take it you guys have a construction business?"

Before Skeeter could answer, he was up at the counter and ordering a large Americano with room for milk, and a cinnamon roll.

When it was her turn to order, Nelly placed the same order as the night before, but added two hard-boiled eggs. She'd need the protein for the day she had ahead of her.

"I'll save you a seat with us," Skeeter offered when he picked up his drink and walked to a table where Mike already sat.

Nelly watched the man walk away and noticed his limp. It didn't bother her that he had some sort of injury, but she wondered if he'd fallen off a horse or a ladder.

After she sat down with her order, Sam also joined them.

Everyone sat there eating and drinking quietly for a few minutes. As the wonderful caffeine from the hot coffee entered her bloodstream, she sighed and her brain began to clear up. Then she realized she knew the names Jerod and Crooked Arrow Ranch.

"You weren't talking about Jerod Stevens, were you?" Nelly wiped her mouth and waited for one of the men to respond before she took another bite of the ooey gooey, delicious, and hot cinnamon roll. It was cooked to perfection, not overdone, and not undercooked, either. The cinnamon and vanilla icing dripped from eat bite she took, making a mess of her mouth and fingers, even though she used a knife and fork.

Sam glared at Skeeter before answering. "Yes, do you know Jerod?"

Nelly shook her head. "Not really. We've messaged each other a few times and had numerous phone calls. I wasn't supposed to arrive until next weekend. Now I know why." Her original plans had been to leave a week later, but she found herself too anxious to get started on setting up her house and kennels so she'd left as soon as the house closed escrow.

Mike tilted his head and stared, but said nothing.

It was Skeeter who spoke first. "How do you know Jerod? Are you coming to work at the ranch, too?"

"Not exactly." Nelly was being intentionally cryptic. Until she spoke with Jerod, she didn't want to say what her relationship with the ranch was going to be. "But you guys—excuse me, *cowboys*—do construction on old, dank, and disgusting houses?" While she wasn't ready to laugh over her situation yet, a corner of her lips turned up just enough to make it look like a smile.

"We help where we can." Sam didn't look at her; instead, he stuffed the burrito into his mouth and ate.

Speaking of cryptic, Nelly took another bite of her cinnamon roll and followed it up with a sip of her black coffee. Then she asked what he meant by his comment.

"What he means," Skeeter interjected, "is that our ranch isn't the typical one in these here parts. We take on odd jobs where we can while we learn how to run a ranch."

Nelly knew exactly what the Crooked Arrow Ranch did. However, Jerod hadn't said much about working odd jobs. He had told her they would help around the county where they could, but that was about it.

"Well, I have a meeting with Jerod a week from Monday. But until then, I do have a lot of work to do on the house. As it stands it's a health hazard, and probably a health violation as well. I'm surprised escrow closed on it with the house in such bad shape." She was also still upset with the Realtor for not disclosing the dangerous shape it was in.

"I've heard about the house," Sam said. "I'm glad you aren't living in it. But where are you staying?"

"The barn."

All three heads turned to her in shock.

Skeeter looked dumbfounded and his fork clanked to the table. "Surely that's even worse then the house, right?"

Nelly giggled. Never had she seen three men all give her the same exact look of fear mixed with confusion. "The barn is in fantastic shape, almost as though someone knew I was coming and would need a safe place to stay, so they fixed it up."

"Huh, sounds like you might have a guardian angel." Skeeter picked his fork up and began eating again.

"That's what I thought, too." Nelly looked up and sent a silent thanks to God.

"So, what are ya gonna do?" Sam asked between bites of his burrito.

What Nelly wanted to say was that she was going to head over to the Realtor's office and tear into him for keeping this from her. She wasn't familiar with Montana real estate law, but surely they had laws against fraud like this, right? But what she said was, "I'm going to have a nice conversation with the pig who sold me the ranch and see what he's going to do to help fix the situation."

Sam shook his head. "Good luck. And when you're done, come see us. We can help at a very reasonable rate."

After getting Sam's contact information, Nelly got up and headed to Missoula, where her rat of a Realtor worked.

*Chapter 4*

S am watched as Nelly left the coffee shop. "She's gonna be trouble, ain't she."

The moment Sam and the guys made it back to the ranch, they were put to work and didn't have a moment to even think about Nelly. Wedding preparations took all day long, then Sam had to shower and put on his monkey suit. The entire time he readied, he did nothing but complain.

"All I'm doing is helping people find their seats. Why do I need to dress up? This is a ranch wedding, for Pete's sake. We should all be in our denim and boots. Maybe a nicer button-up shirt with a bolo tie, but that should be all." Sam complained to anyone who would listen, but everyone just smiled and shook their heads. Anyone who'd been around the ranch for at least a month knew Sam was more hot air than anything else.

But the moment Sam saw Dana in her wedding dress at the end of the aisle, and then turned to see Jerod all teary-eyed, his complaints stopped. While he wouldn't be caught dead marrying anyone, he did know Jerod and Dana were madly in love and they deserved their day. Sam wasn't about to begrudge them their happiness.

As Dana walked down the aisle, Sam felt a tickle in the back of his throat and then his nose burned. He clamped his eyes shut and thought about mucking out stalls. No way was he going to get emotional over someone else's wedding, even if it was the joining of two of the nicest folks he'd ever met. Sam had never seen two people more suited to each other.

It'd been about a year since they'd met. At first, Sam wondered what Dana saw in Jerod. The cowboy wasn't much nicer than Sam. Well, that wasn't true. Jerod was one of those cowboys who would literally give someone in need the shirt off his back.

When Sam opened his eyes again, Dana and Jerod were holding hands under the arbor where the preacher stood. While his hearing was just fine, no thanks to the bombs that went off all around him when we was in the Middle East, he couldn't hear the words the preacher spoke over the sound of rushing water in his head.

It took running his hands down his face a few times and then shaking his head to clear up the noise. Sam was just grateful he had a seat in the back of the crowd. His throat was tight and a headache had begun, but after a few seconds he got himself under control.

The panic attacks had lessened a great deal since Dana had arrived and worked with him, but crowds and loud noises still weren't his thing. If he had been up front, he was sure he'd have passed out from all the eyes on him. That was the worst thing, ever.

When people stared at his arm and he saw the look of realization on their faces, he got mad. But when it happened in front of a large group, he got dizzy. Sam knew what they were all thinking...he was half the man he once was. And they all had that look of pity in their eyes. The look that said they wanted to tell him everything would be alright.

But everything *wouldn't* be alright. Nothing would ever be alright.

His mind jerked back to the parade, a happier time before he'd left for war.

Some called out his name and said how proud they were to have one of their own joining the war on terror. But that was over ten years ago, when Americans had spirit. When they loved their country and their servicemembers. Sure, even today there were still a lot who had a patriotic spirit, but lately it had become unfashionable to support the military, or even the police. And that hurt.

Not just because Sam had planned on being a police officer when he exited the service, but because his exit wasn't the way he'd planned it. And now that dream of working hard to keep his hometown safe would never happen.

*He* would never happen.

Who would want a shell of a man patrolling their streets? One who didn't even have all of his limbs? No, Sam was no longer a real man, and the atmosphere in his country only made it worse.

Now he was a shell of what he once was, and no one even cared.

An elbow nudged him in the ribs, and he scowled at Mike.

Mike smiled and pointed to the happy couple who had turned around. Somehow, he had missed the entire service. Sam didn't even get to hear them both say, "I do." He stood when everyone else did and clapped for the newlyweds.

All of the pictures and speeches had taken so long that by the time he finally ate, Sam's stomach was growling more than he was. Sam walked over to a group of the residents from the ranch. "Hey, does this mean we're done for the night?"

Dixon, one of the vets who also lived at the ranch, grinned and shook his head. "Nope, now it's time to take everything down."

Grumbling, Sam got to work folding chairs and putting them in the back of a big box truck. They had rented all the party furniture the wedding needed, and now they had to get it back to the rental company.

"Congratulations, Jerod and Dana. I do wish you the best." Sam finally smiled at the wedding couple and wished them well when they took off to a hotel in Missoula for their wedding night. The next day, they were headed to Florida for their honeymoon.

Once the happy couple left, Sam turned to Skeeter. "Who does their honeymoon at Disney World? Why not take a cruise, or rent a beach house?"

It was Thursday by the time Sam heard from Nelly again. And that was only by accident.

"Sam? Is that you?" Nelly stared at the clean-shaven man who had resembled more of a mountain man than a cowboy when she met him.

Sam had just put his hot cup of joe to his lips and was about to take a sip from the nectar of the gods. Instead, he turned around to stare into the deep brown pools of Nelly Wilson's eyes and his heart dropped into his stomach. His eyes widened and he heard himself ask, "When did she get so pretty?"

When Nelly's cheeks turned a bright shade of pink, he realized his mistake. After speaking mostly to himself for the past two years, he had gone and gotten himself into trouble by uttering his thoughts aloud. Thoughts no one wanted to hear.

Trying to think of something to say, he took a long drink of his coffee and sputtered it out when it burned his esophagus. "So sorry."

A brown stain was already making its way down the front of Nelly's shirt. Sam reached for a stack of napkins and dabbed at the mess until she swatted his hand away.

"Just want do you think you're doing?" Nelly put her hands in front of her chest.

A growl emanated from a dog standing next to her, baring his teeth at Sam.

"Whoa, now. I didn't mean anything by it." Sam put his hands in the air and stepped back two paces, more to put room between him and Nelly than him and the dog. The one thing he still enjoyed was animals, and they usually took an instant liking to him as well.

But now? He'd probably made two enemies for life. What was new?

Nelly put her hand, palm down, in front of the dog next to her. "Fuss."

Sam had heard that command many times in the field. He narrowed his eyes and took another look at the dog next to Nelly. He was a service dog, and he was on duty. The dog had a desert camo vest on with the words *SERVICE DOG* embroidered on the sides. He knew from his time in the sandpit that any time a dog had on one of those vests, it meant he was working and no one should come up to the dog. He wasn't a pet, he was an employee.

Sam gave a nod to the dog, who'd probably served himself. Maybe he was semi-retired now? Nelly didn't have the look of a soldier, so he wasn't sure why she had a military service dog next to her. But he'd be sure to give her and the dog a wide berth moving forward. The dog was a beautiful black retriever with white spots on his head, and they usually had an easygoing temperament. But the military dogs were also trained to protect their handlers. If he wasn't careful, he'd have this dog taking a chunk out of his leg. Or worse, pulling his prosthetic arm out of his shirt sleeve.

Nelly turned her soft brown eyes on him and sighed. "I know, Sam. It's just"—her arms flailed in front of her—"this has been one awful week. It's probably a good thing I came early, but at the same time, I wish Jerod was here so we could get started."

Sam tilted his head. "Started on what? Your ranch? I told you, I can help you while Jerod's on his honeymoon. Should I come over this afternoon and take a look at what you need?"

# Chapter 5

The last thing Nelly wanted, or needed, was company. And certainly not from a single cowboy who made her heart pitter-patter. But she hadn't made much progress on the house.

Spike growled again, and Nelly looked down. "Sitz," she commanded, and Spike sat on his haunches. However, he didn't take his eyes off Sam, and Nelly had to stifle a laugh. A woman had to appreciate a dog who looked out for her. Spike would pair nicely with a female. When the time came to place Spike with a patient, she'd have to look for a woman to work with Spike. He tended to dislike men.

"I see you've got a military service dog. How'd that happen?" Sam didn't smile at the dog, but he didn't frown, either. Which was unusual for the grumpy guy.

Nelly had noticed he always wore a glove on his left hand, but not on his right. His left arm was also not quite right. But since he wore a long-sleeve shirt every time she saw him, she couldn't know what the problem was. One thought that came to her was that he'd been in a fire. Or at least his arm had. That could account for why he was always keeping the skin covered—horrible burn scars.

Not that she minded either way. But she knew how cruel people could be. Most wouldn't say a thing, but the way people stared at anyone who was different was just as bad as saying something rude.

"Actually, I'm a trainer. I have four dogs at the moment, and should be receiving more once I get one of my dogs placed." There, she'd said it. Nelly knew from past experience that in small towns, word got around faster than a speeding bullet. However, she didn't want everyone to know who was going to be receiving a dog until the veteran knew.

Sam's eyes rose, and he took another look at the dog next to her. Then he narrowed his eyes and glared at Nelly. "And just who's gettin' your dogs?"

Nelly wasn't going to let this unruly wannabe cowboy get her goose. She could give back just as good as she got. "That is none of your business." She almost said something about patient confidentiality, but shut her mouth before she could utter another word. Until Jerod returned, she'd keep the fact that her dogs were all here to work with the wounded vets a secret.

Sam grunted. "Is this why you're here in Frenchtown?"

"I moved to Frenchtown because I thought I was getting a good deal on a small ranch. One that had the exact space I needed and was located next to a main highway." Exasperated already by her encounter with Sam, she sighed. "Look, I'm exhausted and really don't want to argue with you."

"Yeah, yeah. I get it." Sam scratched his chin. "So, do you need some help with that train wreck of a house?"

Nelly practically snorted. "Train wreck? I wish it was that good." She rubbed her hand down her face and looked to Spike, who seemed to have relaxed his posture just a bit. "It's bad. I don't know if it would be better to just tear it down and start over."

"Did rats get into all the walls?" A faraway look entered Sam's eyes, and Nelly wondered if he'd had a similar experience before.

"Not all. But the rats wouldn't be so bad if it were just them. Something pretty big must have crawled into a wall somewhere and died. I just can't find it. And I do need to get an exterminator out." She shook her head and wished she'd come out to see the house first. If she had, she would have passed on this one. But it was in the right location. Had she not taken this one, she would have been over an hour away from the Crooked Arrow Ranch. Which wouldn't have been ideal.

"We can help," was all Sam said.

Nelly waited for more details, but when he stayed quiet she asked a few more questions. The biggest one was about costs. "Look, I don't have much money yet. I'm waiting for a few more grants to come through, so I don't know how much I can afford."

Sam nodded. "Well, how about I take a look and then we can talk? Jerod is usually pretty soft on payment terms." He looked down at the dog. "Maybe he can even work out some sort of swap."

Nelly looked down at Spike. "Ah, I don't know about that. But, I do think having a carpenter at the very least take a look would be a good idea."

"You say you're sleeping out in the barn? How's that working out?" A tiny smile edged up one side of his face, almost as though he'd had a stroke and couldn't fully smile anymore.

"Pretty good, but I could use a stove and a couple of other items. I was planning on heading over to the general store today to see what I could find." What she really wanted was a secondhand store, but there weren't any in town.

"Why don't you hold off on any purchases until we take a look?" Sam nodded and then headed toward the door.

"Wait, where are you going?" Nelly turned, confusion covering her face. They hadn't set up a time for him to come see the house yet.

"Why, I'm heading to your ranch. You comin'?" Sam looked back over his shoulder expectantly.

"Hold your horses, I need coffee and a cinnamon roll." Nelly shook her head and got back in line.

"Hi, Nelly. Good to see you again. The usual?" Lottie, the proprietress of the best coffee shop in town—well, the only coffee shop in town—greeted Nelly with a smile and a hot cinnamon roll.

"Thanks, you're a life-saver." Nelly paid for her breakfast and took the offered coffee and warm roll.

Sam was waiting outside for Nelly. "Why don't I follow you to the ranch?"

"Sure." Nelly took a large bite out of her cinnamon roll and jumped in her truck after putting Spike in the back.

As she drove up the dirt lane leading to the house, Nelly shivered and wished she didn't have to go back inside the house. Two days ago she'd given Lank, the Realtor, what for. But he'd just smiled and said she should have come to see the property for herself. Then he went on to say he had no idea the house was in such bad condition. Then a bunch of platitudes, nothing that would actually help her. Since then, she'd been inside trying to find what had died and left that horrendous stench.

She stopped her truck just outside the house and waited for Sam.

"I should warn you, it's pretty awful. You might want a bandana to cover your nose or something." Nelly took her own advice and put a cloth over her nose and mouth once she had Spike ready to go. Since her first steps inside the house, she hadn't entered again without at least one dog at her side.

The moment Sam entered the house, his eyes began to water and he coughed. Once he was adjusted to the environment, he looked around the living room. "Whoa, I've never seen anything like this. It looks as though whoever used to live here was a packrat, or hoarder. What made you buy this place?"

She snorted. "Well, lesson learned. Never buy a house without inspecting it for yourself. I trusted that the pictures the Realtor sent me were accurate and up to date. They must have been twenty years old."

"Yeah, I wouldn't suggest doing that again." Sam rubbed the back of his neck and shivered. "Well,

I'd say the first thing that needs to be done is bring in a forty-yard dumpster to clear out the place. Until it's cleared, I really can't tell you what all needs to be done."

"I was afraid of that." While she had him there, she might as well ask a few questions. "What do you think died in here? I've looked around a bit but can't find it."

Sam walked around and sniffed a few times, trying to locate the source of the stench. He pointed to the broken window, then walked toward the stairs. "Have you been upstairs yet?"

She shook her head. "No way. I wasn't about to get stuck upstairs with whatever, or whoever, caused this disaster."

Sam chuckled. It was a deep, sexy sound that caught Nelly's attention. She had barely seen the man smile; she didn't think he'd ever laugh. Well, it wasn't actually a laugh, but close enough to make her want to hear a real laugh from him.

"You afraid of what you might find up there?" He nodded up the stairs.

"You betcha. I'm afraid I might find a dead body." Nelly waved her hands in front of her. "No thank you."

When Sam looked at her, his eyes seemed as though he wanted to ask her a question, but he didn't. Instead he climbed over the rubble blocking the staircase.

From what Nelly could see, there were stacks of newspapers lined up around two of the walls that went from floor to ceiling. Clothes littered the floor, but not the sort that could be cleaned and used again. No, most of the items were in tatters and covered in filth. She had seen those reality shows about hoarders and knew that this house had to be the worst one ever. A dead human upstairs wouldn't surprise her.

When Sam was halfway up, he looked down. "You comin'?"

She shook her head. "No, I'm fine right here."

This time, Sam did laugh. "Come on, I'll protect you. And if I can't, that mean dog by your side will."

Spike growled and showed his teeth as though he knew exactly what Sam had said and didn't like it. Nope, not one bit.

It was Nelly's turn to laugh. "I don't think Spike likes you."

"Spike, ha? The name suits him." Sam turned and headed upstairs.

Nelly took a deep breath, coughed it back out, and headed upstairs. She turned to see Spike sitting where she'd left him and rolled her eyes heavenward. She patted her thigh, then commanded, "Hier."

Spike grudgingly followed with his tail between his legs. The dog was trained to do as commanded, but that didn't mean he was going to like it.

When Nelly and Spike where halfway up the stairs, they heard Sam yelling, "Oh, that's just wrong."

Nelly's eyebrows shot up past her bangs and she looked to Spike just as the dog twisted his head to look at his handler. They both stopped. "Is everything alright up there?" Nelly called out. She wasn't about to keep going if Sam was going to bolt back downstairs.

"Watch where you step. Large animals have been up here." The irritation in Sam's voice conveyed all she needed to know.

When a tinkle of a laugh escaped, she clamped a hand over her mouth.

"You laugh now, but just wait until you step in it," Sam growled.

Spike barked when he got to the top of the stairs, and the humor in Nelly's face evaporated. Upstairs looked more like a war zone than a house.

"Are those holes from gunshots?" Nelly put a hand up to one hole, then pulled it back. She didn't need to be touching anything.

A loud crash and an expletive came from a room down the hall.

"Sam, are you alright?" When she didn't hear a reply, she looked to Spike and pointed to where she thought the sound came from. "Such," she said, the command for track. The German pronunciation was nothing like how it was spelled. While it was spelled *such*, it was actually pronounced *zook*.

Spike began his search, sniffing and looking into the doors, but not entering a room. He knew Sam's scent, and he also instinctively knew to look for the man, even though Spike didn't like him. Nelly had trained her dogs well, and they were quite obedient.

When Spike found his mark, he entered quietly and searched for only a second before he barked. Nelly made her way through the debris to find Spike sniffing Sam, who was laying on a pile of trash.

"Go ahead, laugh. But just remember, this is your dump to clean." Sam started to move, but Spike was still hovering over him, sniffing.

"Spike, Platz." The command for down was easily obeyed, and the dog moved away from Sam, giving him enough room to stand up.

"What happened? Why'd you fall?" Nelly looked around but couldn't see anything that could cause him to trip and fall. Then she noticed what he was staring at and she almost fell backward herself when she tried to move away.

Spike sniffed, but didn't bark or react. He knew what it was, and that it wasn't a threat.

"Is it dead?" Nelly leaned forward, then jerked her head back as the stench wafted closer to her nose.

"Yeah, and it looks like it's been here for a while. I'm betting that's what caused the smell, or at least most of it." Sam waved around the room. "I'm sure there's plenty more carcasses around, but the dead bear is most likely the main cause."

Slumped in the corner of the room were the remains of a black bear.

# Chapter 6

Sam had seen a lot in his time. He'd gone hunting before, but not for bear. And he'd seen plenty of death in the Middle East during his two tours. But this was different. While he'd heard plenty of stories about mutilations, he'd never actually seen it up close before. "I think the bullet holes throughout the house were from local kids goofing off. They must have killed the bear and then shot it up with everything they had left to make sure it stayed down."

Nelly's face turned white as a sheet, and Sam worried she'd pass out. This wasn't a place to fall down; he knew from his own trip.

"Nelly, let's get downstairs. You don't need to see this and neither does your dog." Sam nodded to the dog and slowly walked toward Nelly. If she was about to pass out he wanted to be close enough to catch her, but he didn't want the dog to bite him for helping her.

"Right, I think I've seen enough." Nelly turned, and without a word Spike followed her out and down the stairs. They didn't stop until they were outside on the dirt.

Nelly put a hand on the dog's head and scratched. "Braver Hund. Good dog."

Sam watched in amazement as Nelly and her dog communicated. He knew from his time in Afghanistan what she was saying to Spike, and that he was trained well. Something about her connection to Spike warmed his heart just enough to keep his mind off what he'd seen in the house.

When Nelly was composed, she stood up straight and looked at the house without any emotion showing on her face. "So, do you think I can hire a company to come in and clean the place up? Or at least get all of that junk out of there? And what about the bear?" When she finished rattling off her questions, she turned her head to look at Sam.

The sun was behind Nelly, and it glinted off the red highlights in her hair in such a way as to create a halo over her head. She was beautiful. He had to stop this train of thought. Instead, he thought about the room upstairs and his mind went back to Nelly's reaction.

He'd never seen such a strong woman before. When he saw the bear carcass, he almost peed himself. And if she hadn't been there, just down the hall, he might have puked as well. Something inside him knew he couldn't do that with her in earshot and maintain what little manhood he had left. So, he felt the churning in his stomach and willed it to stop.

"Sam? Hello, Earth to Sam." Nelly waved a hand in front of his face.

"Oh, sorry." He shook his head. "What?"

Nelly chuckled. "I get it. The place is pretty gross. I almost got lost in my thoughts too." She sobered up when she noticed the grim expression on his face. "Are you alright?"

Sam cleared his throat. "I'm fine. What were you asking?" He didn't want to go into why he'd zoned out. It had started when he saw how beautiful she was with the sun shining behind her. Then when he thought about upstairs, well, he didn't want to go into it. Sam had thought he'd gotten past his PTSD, but something about the sight brought back a flash of memory. One he'd rather not remember.

Megan had told him there would be times when the strangest things would bring back a bad memory, but until today he could easily justify anything that had brought back the nightmare that was war. When he was in Afghanistan, he'd never seen anything like this. No one had enough junk to toss out, or hoard, like the person had done here. So it made no sense why a dead animal brought him back to the carnage he'd tried so hard to forget.

"Do you want to have a cup of tea? Or coffee? I can make either back in the barn. Plus it smells so much better in the barn than it does out here." She chuckled. "Imagine that, a barn smelling better than a house." Nelly waved him toward the vehicles so they could drive to where the barn was located.

While the walk was close, Sam agreed that parking the trucks by the barn would be better. He didn't want to walk back to the house and smell the stench again. Shoot, he didn't even want to clean that place up. If it were up to him, he'd bulldoze the place and start from scratch. Maybe even start on a whole new foundation and bury this one.

Once they were inside the barn, Sam began to relax and feel better. The flashing images of war had fled and he could take in the barn. "Whoa, you must have spent all day and night getting this place in shape."

Nelly sat next to him and took a sip of her coffee before speaking. "No, it was locked up tight and super clean. It seemed like someone had come through and tidied it all up just for me."

After Sam took a sip of his coffee, he furrowed his brows. "Was it the Realtor?"

"I doubt it. When I spoke to him about the house, he never once mentioned the state of the barn. And he told me he'd not been out here. It must have been where the owner was living." She looked around and smiled when she spotted her dogs in their kennels. "Do you mind if I let the dogs out?"

Sam snorted and thought of that song. In his head he sang the line to himself and woofed. Then he turned to look at her and nodded. "Sure, as long as you can promise they won't bite me."

A sly grin spread across her face. "Oh, I don't know about that. But I can say that as long as you're on your best behavior, the dogs will be, too."

Sam liked her. She had a great sense of humor. It was a bit dark, like his. "Well, just so you know, if they bite me, I bite back."

Nelly laughed and shook her head as she headed toward the horse stalls she had set up as the kennel area. "Something tells me you bite first."

When Sam got the double meaning, his cheeks warmed. If only he could be so lucky.

Once the dogs had come out of the kennels and looked Sam up and down, they left and went to the fenced-in area Nelly had set up for them to stretch their legs in.

"I'm impressed by how much you've done since arriving." Sam took another sip of his cooling coffee. "How much have you done here in the barn?"

"Actually, I've only fenced in the paddock area so the dogs can go out there without me tagging along. Well, I've also set up personal stuff, but like I said, the barn was all ready for us when I arrived. It was almost as though someone was living here. Which is why I think it was the owner. He probably moved out here when the house..." Nelly pointed in the direction of the house. "Well, whatever happened there."

"I don't think that was a quick situation. And I don't think it was the owner living out here. He died a couple years back and the place sat empty for a while. Which was why the neighbors were able to buy off portions of the land." Sam stood up to top off his coffee. "Would you like a warm-up?"

Nelly's face heated and she looked away.

Sam felt his neck blazing with fire and he mumbled. "Not what I meant." He cleared his throat. "I mean, would you like a top off for your coffee?"

Sam watched as Nelly lowered her head and bit her lower lip. She nodded.

He couldn't have been happier to leave a room. The tension was building between them, something he'd not felt since...well, a long time. And it wasn't something he wanted happening. Shoot, she probably hadn't noticed his missing arm yet. Once she did, she'd give him that look of pity, say it didn't bother her, and then a few weeks down the road she'd leave him because she didn't want someone who wasn't a whole man.

When he topped off his coffee, he stood there trying to calm his nerves. He was a soldier and he knew how to be professional. This little lady wasn't about to break through the cinderblock walls, chain-link fence, and several rows of claymore mines he'd erected around his heart. No siree, he wasn't going to let another woman tell him he wasn't man enough for her.

With his new resolve in place, he picked up the coffee pot and walked out to top off her mug.

"Thank you, Sam. I appreciate you coming all this way and...well...surviving that monstrosity of a house." She screwed up her lips. "No, that's not a house. It's a horror house."

Sam chuckled. "Too bad Halloween is so far off. You could open it up and charge admission. Just attempting to walk through that place would be enough to make a fortune. Then you could afford to tear it down and start over."

"That would be a great idea! But do you think we'd lose very many kids? I can't imagine too many would find their way out." Nelly grinned.

"You mean like one of those escape rooms?" Sam had heard of locking people into a room with lots of clutter and the guests had to find a way out, but it never sounded like fun to him.

Her face lit up with excitement, and she pointed to him and then her nose. "Exactly! We could make money year-round with an escape room that taunted thrill-seekers with a bear carcass and real bullet holes all over the house. We could even give prizes to anyone who removed a live rat."

"I see. You want people to pay good money to be scared senseless in your...house. And then also reward them for doing your pest control for you?" He could see where she was going with this, and while the idea was hilarious, the house looked as though it really would swallow up anyone who entered.

Nelly waved a hand in front of her. "I know, I know. But it was a nice thought." She put her coffee mug down on the table in front of her. "How much do you think it'll cost to clear the house of all the junk, and the dead bodies?"

"Well, animal control will come out and take the bear free of charge. That's a health hazard and since it's a protected species, they'll want to check it all out." Sam knew there wouldn't be any trouble for Nelly, but animal control could be particular when it came to bears. It was best not to try and hide it.

"Okay, so number one on the list, get animal control out here. Then contact a pest control company?" Her furtive glance at Sam let him know she was in way over her head.

Sam rubbed his chin. It was gonna take some time getting used to a clean-shaven face, but that was what he got for making a bet and losing it.

Shoot, how was he to know that Mike Blankenship's date was real, and not a lady who just felt sorry for him? How in the world Mike, the man who barely said two words a day, found the time and the words to get a woman go actually go out on a date with him, Sam would never know. Sadly, his face was paying the price for his stubbornness.

"Actually, I think the first thing to do is have everyone who wants to help get a tetanus shot, and that includes you, dog whisperer." If anyone heard the way Sam was talking to Nelly, he'd be labeled a flirt. Maybe not on the same level as Skeeter, but sakes alive, he was on a roll today.

"Better than a bear whisperer," Nelly shot back.

Was she flirting with him? No, Sam needed to get a hold of himself and tell his heart to shove off a cliff. He wasn't about to do anything with that woman.

Or was he?

"Well, I think I'll head back to the ranch and see who's up for a deadly assignment." Sam winked and stood up. "Once I know who all can help, I'll call you and give you a price."

Nelly interrupted. "But I don't have any money at the moment. Well, not enough to pay for labor, at any rate." She looked down at her hands.

"Like I said, payment can wait until you get one of those grants." He turned and looked toward the house. "Besides, I think we really need to clean that place out. It's a real health hazard, and I know Jerod well enough to know that if he knew what it was like, he'd have had it cleaned out before you arrived."

With a grimace, Nelly stood and put out her hand, palm up.

Sam furrowed his brow. "What? You want to slap hands?" He didn't understand what she was putting her hand out for. It wasn't like he was going to pay her money.

A light giggle escaped Nelly's lips. "No, silly. Give me your phone and I'll input my contact details."

A light went off in his head. It had been so long since a pretty woman wanted to give him her number, he wasn't expecting it. "Sure, of course." He handed her his phone and once she input her info, she sent herself a text message.

"There, now we have each other's contact info. Let me know when you have some numbers together and when you can wrangle some men to come help. Then I'll arrange for the dumpster to come." Nelly pulled on her ear. "Do you think anything in that death trap is worth saving?"

"Nah, I'd bet animals have left their mark on everything. You don't want the hassle of any of it. Besides, I didn't see anything that was in good enough condition to salvage and repair." He had looked. One item looked like it might have been alright, until he opened the door to the wardrobe and noticed the stain inside. He guessed several animals had used it as their toilet.

"Thanks, I really appreciate it." Nelly walked him to his truck and waved as he drove away.

Sam looked in the rearview mirror and felt a sense of danger fill his entire being. "That woman's gonna be the death of me." He grinned. "But what an adventure it could be."

# Chapter 7

M ost people wouldn't think spending time with a man in a hoarder's nest would create an attraction, but somehow, Nelly couldn't get Sam off her mind. Sure, his reaction to the bear was hilarious, but he was also sweet and helpful. He seemed like a real man, not one of those pretty boys who'd cry at seeing a dead mouse.

Of course, the fact that Sam was sexy as sin didn't hurt matters, either. While most women preferred their men with a sunnier disposition, Nelly knew that deep down he was a good guy and could smile and laugh. He just needed someone to coax it out of him. Although, she had always liked the brooding sort.

Rogue padded up next to her.

"What do you think, boy? Is he a good guy?" Nelly knew the dogs couldn't really understand her when she asked questions like that. They only knew short commands. But her dogs weren't dumb. No, they were very smart. And at times she would have sworn they knew exactly what was going on.

Rogue gave a little chuff and turned in a circle with his tongue lolling to one side.

Nelly knew this meant Rogue was ready for some play time. Even though they were working dogs, they also needed their play time. Just like humans did. She tried to keep work all in German, but when they played, she spoke to them in English. It might not be the best way to train the dogs, but it did help them decipher work from play.

As she turned to head outside, she smiled at the boxer keeping up with her. "Who's a good boy?" Rogue chuffed, and she stopped to scratch his head. "That's right, you're a good boy."

But she had to remind herself that she wasn't here to meet men. She was here to further her business. Before coming to Montana, she'd lived in the Atlanta, Georgia area. Her cousin had a little farm southeast of the city limits where she was able to start her business. Nelly had already successfully placed six service dogs with owners who needed their help. When she left, she'd heard that all six of those patients were doing so much better since getting their dogs.

While she wanted to help everyone in need, her main goal was to help veterans. She had a special relationship with them and it hurt her to no end every time she heard the story of a servicemember or veteran committing suicide. It reminded her of her brother. She wasn't about to let another man or woman fall into such a depression that they couldn't get back out.

No, instead she had decided to apply for government grants that would allow her to build up her business and place service dogs for free with any veteran who needed one. Which was why she was in Frenchtown instead of Atlanta.

Well, an ex-boyfriend might have also been a good reason to leave town. But she wasn't going to dwell on Mick.

Instead, she spent the next hour playing with the dogs. Throwing their favorite toys for them to fetch, or playing tug of war with knotted ropes. These dogs loved their toys, and Nelly loved these dogs.

That night, after a supper of crock pot stew, Sam called her and when she saw his name on the caller ID, her hands shook. Part of it was nerves over the cost of just cleaning the place out, but the other part was talking to Sam. She had to get ahold of her emotions. It would do her no good to like a man at the moment; she needed to focus everything she had on her business and getting that rats' nest of a house cleaned out.

A deep, sultry voice on the other line had butterflies zooming around Nelly's stomach. "Hey Nelly, it's Sam."

Like she didn't know who it was. She rolled her eyes and the butterflies began to dissipate. "Hi, Sam. How goes it?"

"Fair to middling." He cleared his throat and the line went dead for a few seconds. "Uh, how are you doing? Staying clear of that danger zone?"

She chuckled. Sam was sweet. It figured the first thing he'd ask about was her safety. "Ah, yeah. I'm fine. And no worries, I'm not even touching that house until we get some people over here to clean it out. I've seen enough to know there's no way

I'm heading back in there by myself." She shivered just thinking of what all might be crawling around, and what might already be dead.

"I'm just glad the place isn't haunted." Sam chuckled. "Well, at least I don't think it is. Have you seen specters hanging around at night?"

Nelly easily smiled and relaxed her shoulders. He had a good sense of humor. Or at least, one she understood. "That would be a hard negative. No ghosts here. If there were, the dogs would scare them off."

"Too true, too true." His voice became serious again as he went on to discuss business. "I think we should plan for the dumpster to arrive on Monday and I'll have at least six guys help. I'll call the local department of wildlife and see if they want to come over before we start to junk the place, or once we have a safer path for them to walk through."

"Great, and I'll be sure to have enough hazmat suits for everyone to stay safe." She couldn't help it —she had to get one last little joke in. Although, it would be best to ensure she had plenty of work gloves and masks. Even goggles wouldn't be out of the question. Who knew what all would be flying around the air in that place once they began moving stuff?

"Sounds good. Why don't you call me after you've made arrangements for the dumpster, and if I don't hear from you before I speak with the Department of Wildlife, I'll call you."

Sam continued to tell her the rates they would charge and reiterated that she could pay once she had her grant money.

"Are you sure Jerod will be alright with that? I don't want you to get in trouble for making promises he doesn't want to keep." Nelly nibbled on her lower lip, unsure if she should tap into her credit card cash advance line, or wait until she had the grant money before doing anything. "Should we just wait for Jerod to get home and see what he says?"

A relaxed reply from Sam helped to ease her conscience just a bit more. "Nah, no need to wait. I think it's important we get that place cleaned up as soon as possible. It's a danger to not only you, but the dogs."

"I know, you're right. I just hate accepting your work without having the money to pay right away." While she could tap into her credit cards, she didn't want to start charging things she couldn't pay off at the end of the month. She'd learned her lesson with using credit cards and didn't want to get back into old, bad habits. It was never a good thing to spend money before you had it.

And while she wasn't exactly using a credit card, she was in a sense spending money she didn't yet have.

"Listen, Jerod will probably say no pay was needed. All of us here at the ranch have to do so many hours of community service a month. And let me tell you, this would definitely qualify as community service." Sam went on to tell her about some of the assignments they'd had.

"Wow, sounds like you've been at the ranch a long time. Are you a patient or an employee?" While Nelly knew the history of the ranch, and that most of the men there were recovering wounded vets, she also knew some were actual ranch hands. They did have a need for experienced ranchers to help run the place and train the returning vets on ranch life.

The gruff voice from when she'd first met Sam was back. "I've been here about eighteen months. I think I know a thing or two about how Jerod runs the place."

Nelly instantly felt awful. She should have never asked about his status. That was rude and quite frankly none of her business. She just wanted to make sure Sam wasn't committing Jerod to something he wouldn't like. Since she'd never met the man who owned the ranch in person, she wasn't sure what to do.

"Of course, I'm sorry." Nelly shook her head and sighed. "Thank you so much for all of your help. I'll be sure to call the waste management company first thing in the morning."

"Good. Until then, what are you planning to do about cooking?"

"Ah, I was going to see if the general store had a small stove I could buy for the barn. Maybe even a camp stove?" She wasn't sure what would work best. All she knew was that she'd already cooked every recipe she had in the crock pot. She was living on leftovers now, but by Sunday she'd need to make something new and didn't relish the idea of microwave meals.

Another manly grunt came over the line. "Why don't you come to dinner at the ranch tonight? We might have something you could use until we can get you set up properly. You won't want a regular stove in the barn. And really, you'll only need a camp stove and barbecue grill for the summer."

"Oh, I don't want to impose. Especially with Jerod and Dana gone." Nelly didn't know how many men were at the ranch, or if there were any women who lived there. She was told that Jerod had two wounded female vets coming soon, but she didn't know when they would arrive. They were the ones she was going to work with to see who paired well with Spike. She was unsure if she would feel awkward about having dinner with a bunch of men, her being the only woman.

"Nonsense. If you're worried about us old vets, don't. We know how to behave." Sam sounded as though he was offended she hadn't immediately accepted his offer.

Nelly was getting mixed signals from the guy. Did he want her to go to dinner with them, or was he begrudgingly asking her? Or did she hurt his feelings somehow? "Okay, if everyone will be fine with me crashing your dinner, I'd love to come." She almost added *to see the ranch*, but thought better of it. If she had offended him, she didn't want to make it worse.

"Good. Dinner's at six o'clock. Feel free to come early so you can meet everyone before we sit down. We normally eat as a group here. But I must warn you, a few of the guys are a little loud." Sam chuckled, starting to sound a little more like what she was coming to know as his congenial side.

The man did seem to have two sides to him. While Nelly didn't mind the curmudgeonly ol' coot side, she preferred the softer side. But she'd never tell him that. Not in a million years.

"Thank you. Should I bring anything?" Although, Nelly wasn't sure what she could bring since all she could do was heat up stuff in the microwave or in a crock pot.

"Only your appetite."

They hung up, and she looked at Rogue sitting in front of her, staring. He tilted his head as though he was thinking, and Nelly rubbed his head right between his eyes. It was Rogue's soft spot. His tail started smacking the ground and a rumble emanated from somewhere deep inside. The dog was more than content, he was happy.

The others came and stood by her as well. They had probably heard Rogue.

"Oh, I see how it is. You all want my attention when you know scratching and petting are involved." Nelly chuckled and reached out to Buffy, who was the closest to her left side. The dog licked her hand and then stood still while Nelly loved up on her, too.

Angel and Spike were impatient while waiting their turn. Spike tried to nudge Rogue aside and Angel tried to nudge Buffy aside. If she had been watching this in a movie, she would have laughed.

"Alright, alright. I only have two hands. Angel and Spike, you gotta wait your turn."

Once she felt she had given Rogue and Buffy enough attention, she called over the other two dogs. And of course, Rogue and Buffy tried to hone in on the attention only after a few seconds.

Chuckling, Nelly was grateful for the four dogs. Living out on a ranch all alone could be lonesome. But with four large dogs who loved attention, she wasn't missing people at the moment.

*Chapter 8*

"**A**lright, you rascals. You better be on your best behavior tonight. We're gonna have company." Sam pointed at Skeeter. "And you, no flirting with Nelly."

"Oh, does someone have a date?" Skeeter teased.

Mike laughed. "Yeah, right. Sam doesn't date."

Dixon got in on the ribbing, and before long all the guys at the ranch were teasing Sam. He did not like where this was heading. He knew the guys too well to believe they would be nice. Oh, they'd be nice to Nelly, but to him? Sam knew he needed to keep an eye on his own back that night.

Even Megan, the counselor at the Crooked Arrow Ranch who lived in the house, got in on the action.

The sound of the doorbell ringing made its way through the kitchen, and Megan's eyes lit. "I'll get it."

As Megan went to answer the door, Skeeter, Dixon, Mike, and even the quiet guy Arthur followed her. Sam slapped a hand over his face and shook his head. He should have known better than to invite her to dinner. But he'd explained many times that afternoon that the poor woman was literally living in her barn and needed a good, homecooked meal. But did any of them take him seriously? Nope.

As the gang all practically trampled Megan getting to the door, Sam remembered how the afternoon had gone and began to regret inviting her over.

They'd all ribbed him for hours that afternoon about having a date. Arthur, who was normally quiet, asked about getting out the candles and leaving Sam and Nelly in the dining room over a candlelit meal. Then of course the rest of the guys piped in.

"I can put on some music," Arthur Landbury offered.

"How about someone play romantic tunes on the piano? I can accompany on the fiddle." Skeeter grinned and slapped Sam's back.

"Skeeter, I don't think anyone wants to hear your fiddle tonight." Megan shook her head and tried not to laugh. When the man played the fiddle, it sounded more like someone running their fingernails down a chalkboard.

The rest of the day went just like that. And now it was time to welcome Nelly to the craziness that was the Crooked Arrow Ranch.

Sam mentally prepared himself for even more teasing and possibly some practical jokes as he heard Megan answer the door. At least she was introducing Nelly to almost everyone. That was one thing he didn't have to worry about.

Anthony Sullivan walked in and grinned. The moment he heard Nelly's footsteps, the cowboy started in. "Looks like your girlfriend is here, and she's mighty pretty." He suggestively raised his eyebrows and looked expectantly at the door to the kitchen, where they both stood.

The cowboy had lost hearing on his left side from an explosion in Afghanistan. Sam couldn't understand how he had known exactly when to start his teasing.

Nelly walked into the kitchen with her cheeks as red as turnips. The poor woman had obviously heard Anthony. Sam knew it wasn't a date, and he hoped she did as well. If he ever asked a woman out again, it wouldn't be to a communal dinner at the ranch, that was for sure.

"Nelly, sorry for the rudeness of my roommates." Sam glared at Anthony. "I really thought they would be on their best behavior for a new neighbor." He hoped she would understand the message he was trying to convey—they weren't dating.

Nelly bit her lower lip and looked from Sam to Anthony.

"Oh, sorry." Sam jumped a little and went to introduce Anthony. "I think you've met everyone else?"

Megan walked in. "Yup, the rest of the gang met her at the door." She glared at Skeeter. "You and I are going to have a talk later about the proper way to greet a lady."

Sam's brows furrowed and a storm began brewing in his eyes. "What did you do?"

Skeeter put his hands up. "Hey, man. I just gave her a hug. That's all." He looked to Nelly for confirmation.

"And he kissed my cheek." Nelly glared at the flirt.

"Ah, come on. Why'd you go and tell Sam that for?" Skeeter slumped, then backed up a few paces as Sam walked toward him.

"You did what?" Sam almost bellowed, but he held himself back.

Realizing what she had started, Nelly got between the two. "It's fine, Sam. Really. No harm, no foul."

Sam pointed to Skeeter. "I don't ever want to hear that you've kissed a girl without her permission."

"Sorry, Nelly. Really I am." Skeeter turned his sad, puppy dog eyes on her. "I just got a little excited, that's all. I won't do it again."

After a cleansing breath, Nelly nodded. "Fine, but just know that if you do it again, I'll punch you."

"And if her dogs see it, boy howdy!" Sam grinned and slapped his good hand against his thigh. "That's something I'd like to see."

Nelly arched a brow and stared at Sam, then crossed her arms over her chest. "You'd like to see Skeeter try and kiss me again?"

The temperature in the room must have dropped ten degrees. Nelly's icy stare sent a chill up Sam's spine. "No, ma'am. I meant I'd like to see your dogs take Skeeter down a peg or two. That's all." He waved his good hand in front of his face.

Sam tended to keep his left arm, the prosthetic one, away from as many eyes as possible. When he could, he'd put it behind his back. In this situation, he had it down at his side.

Her lips twitched, and Nelly's eyes sparkled with mirth. "I might have to use him in training next week."

"Training? What do you do?" Anthony asked, looking from Sam to Nelly. "Sam only told us you moved into what was left of a neighboring ranch."

"Yes, I bought the old Brown ranch. Several of the neighbors bought up all the land except for ten acres. So I have the house, barn, and just enough area to train my dogs." Nelly smiled at Anthony, and a look of pure delight crossed her face as she spoke about the dogs.

"A dog trainer?" Megan asked. "You don't happen to be the one Jerod told me about? You train service dogs?"

The look of utter joy left Nelly's face and she turned to look at Sam. "Uh, yeah. I do."

Sam wasn't sure why she looked so nervous. It wasn't as though she was going to sell her dogs to the Crooked Arrow; they barely made enough to cover the current programs. There was no way they'd be able to buy service dogs. "Come on, let's go sit down to dinner. I'm sure everyone is famished."

A worried look passed between Megan and Nelly. Then Megan took Nelly's arm and whispered something too low for Sam to hear. After that, all talk was about the area and the events coming up.

"Nelly, have you heard about our new flower festival? The Big Sky Christmas Tree Farm is hosting it this year. It'll be their first year to do it, and everyone is very excited." Megan passed the potatoes to Arthur, who took a large serving before passing the dish on.

The dinner was a feast in Sam's opinion. Megan had outdone herself when she learned that Nelly was coming. They had a glazed ham with all the fixings. Sam wasn't about to complain about the lavish meal; they rarely ate this good. They never went without good meals, but this was like a holiday feast. He was already thinking ahead to dessert.

When Nelly took the platter with ham, she put a large slice on her plate. "Actually, I think I saw something about it in town earlier this week. What's the story with the festival?"

"Megan's dating the guy who manages the farm," Skeeter blurted.

The man was beginning to get on Sam's nerves. Skeeter was young, only in his early twenties, but he sure acted more like a teenager than an adult most days.

Nelly raised her brows and looked to Megan for confirmation. Sam gazed at the pretty woman. She'd cleaned up nicely. He liked it when women wore dresses. Not all the time, because ranch life didn't exactly make that possible, but tonight she was wearing a sky blue sundress that accentuated her tan and made the red highlights in her hair stand out. She had paired it with a denim jacket and tan cowgirl boots. Sam thought she'd fit in nicely with the other ladies in town if she kept up this sort of dress for events and church.

Not that Sam attended church, much. He usually went for holidays, but that was it. He and God had an understanding: God would stay out of his life, and Sam wouldn't complain to others about the unfair treatment he got from the deity who was supposed to take care of him, but hadn't.

It seemed to work out quite nicely.

Sam realized he was staring at Nelly and he averted his gaze before anyone could comment on it. Besides, the plate of steamed green beans was being handed to him from his left, and he had to concentrate as he took the plate in his left hand and used his right to stabilize it.

His recovery was very slow-going, but he was beginning to learn how to use his left hand without dropping everything he touched. The phantom pains were almost gone, and he only wished about twice a day that his friend had been the one to survive, and not him. That was a great improvement over the almost constant wish to have died.

All progress was good progress, as Megan was fond of telling him.

Instead of holding the plate in his left hand like most normal people would do, he set it down. Then he dished himself some green beans. When he was ready to pass the plate, he reached his right hand over and picked it up. That made it easier to hand off to Mike, who was sitting on his right.

The last thing he needed was to drop the dish and make a fool of himself in front of a guest. It didn't matter that she was a pretty woman; he didn't notice such things. Not anymore.

However, Sam wanted to put off Nelly discovering he was only half a man as long as possible. He doubted he could keep the charade up past Monday. Since he'd be the one to lead the clean-up team, he would have to work. And at some point, something would happen and Nelly would discover his missing arm.

"Well, this year the Christmas tree farm is experimenting with various ways to bring more tourists to town, and to the farm," Megan said. "They almost lost it last year. But thanks to some very ingenious ways of diversifying at Christmas, they saved it. For now. But they still need to find ways to make more money throughout the year." Megan took a bite of the mashed potatoes and moaned.

"I did that," Skeeter said.

When half the table put their forks down and glared at Skeeter, he reddened. "I mean, uh..." the man continued to stammer as what he said finally hit him. "I didn't mean it that way. Geesh. I know better than to mess with Daniel Caruthers' girlfriend. What I meant to say was that I made the mashed potatoes. The secret to really creamy potatoes is cream."

If Sam had been sitting next to Skeeter, he would have slapped him up the head. The stupid flirt was going to get himself into trouble one of these days.

The rest of the dinner went off without a hitch, and thankfully Skeeter barely said a word after that.

That was until Megan brought in the dessert.

"Sam and I made this right before dinner. In fact, it's still hot." Megan set the homemade apple pie crumble down in the center of the table. "I also have vanilla bean ice cream to go on top."

"Sam? You're joking, right?" Skeeter scoffed and sat back, eyeing the pie with trepidation.

"Hey, Megan's been teaching me a few things about baking and cooking. I'm getting rather good, if I do say so myself." Sam puffed his chest out and smiled at Megan.

The two of them had regular cooking and baking sessions as part of his rehab program. It served two parts—one was to help him to learn how to use his left hand more, and the other was to instill a sense of accomplishment.

For Megan, it had started out rough. More food had to be thrown away than they could afford, but eventually things improved. And she got quite a good laugh out of it most days.

"But, his hand." Skeeter stared at Sam's left arm.

Sam put it under the table and seethed with anger. He was about to grumble something rude when Nelly spoke up.

"It smells divine." Nelly smiled encouragingly at Sam, then over to Megan, who was cutting slices for everyone. "I can't wait to taste that crumble. Did you use real butter, or margarine?"

"Real, of course." Sam had learned that when baking it was best to use real butter and sugar, unless they were preparing something for a group with an allergy or health issues.

Megan put a slice on a plate and held it out for Nelly. "Á la mode?"

"Of course." Nelly took the plate when Megan handed it to her. Then she took a smile bite of the crumble topping and closed her eyes as she relished the sweet, creamy taste of real butter, cinnamon, and sugar. "I think this is going to be my new favorite dessert."

Everyone complimented the two chefs on their delicious dessert, and Sam realized for the first time that he could actually make something, even with a fake arm. Megan had shown him how to hold the bowls and utensils in such a way that he used his left arm to hold a bowl in place while his right would do all the work. He always held the bowl against his body and used the prosthetic arm on his left to hold the bowl in place.

Sam did have some movement of the fake fingers, but it wasn't much. He didn't have a top-of-the-line bionic arm or anything like that, but it also wasn't a wooden one like the Civil War veterans had to use. He wouldn't be relying on his fingers to pick up anything, but his arm was stable enough to use as an assistive device.

Anthony looked at Sam and grinned. "My, my, the tough soldier boy can cook. Who knew? Cheers, mate." He held up his fork as though he was toasting with a glass of champagne.

When the evening was over, Sam offered to walk Nelly to the door. "Listen, I'm sorry if some of the guys were a bit..."

"Over the top?" Nelly tilted her head and a soft smile spread across her face. "Don't worry about it. I'm used to military men and their ways."

"Really? Did you serve?"

Nelly shook her head. "No, I come from a long line of soldiers. I think just about all of the men in my family served at some point. And even my grandmother was a nurse during World War II." She was actually proud of the fact that her family had such a wonderful history of service to her nation. She had wanted to join as well, but had felt the call to work with service dogs even before her brother's injury.

"Have any of them served outside of the Army?" Sam knew that most families chose one service and stuck to it, but some did have a bit of a rivalry. Especially when it came to Army versus Marines.

Nelly thought about it for a moment, then shook her head. "I don't think so. My great-great grandfather was a flyboy for the Army, but that would have been before the Air Force officially formed. So, he might have joined the Air Force in order to fly if that branch of the military had been around. What about you? Do you come from a military family?"

He looked down. His family was more into business and making money than serving their great nation. Sam shook his head. "No, I think I was the first to willingly sign up. I mean, I know I had some distant relatives who served during the two world wars and Vietnam, but they were all drafted."

"Still, service is service. You should be proud of your relatives who served."

Sam hadn't thought of it that way. He had only known that some members of his family were basically forced into service. While he didn't know of any relatives who'd run away from serving, he also didn't know of anyone else who chose to enlist. "Yeah, I guess you're right." While he didn't smile, he did feel a little bit of the weight he'd been carrying lift.

Megan had always said that talking about his past was good for him. But he thought that talking to her, Megan, was what she meant. Even though he and Nelly didn't discuss injuries or battle, just knowing that she understood the military brought them closer. It was a connection that could never be severed.

"Thank you for inviting me over tonight. This was fun, and the best I've eaten in a long time." She patted her stomach. "I think I'll be working off that dessert for the next few days." Nelly chuckled.

Her lighthearted spirit made him feel good. Sam enjoyed being around her. There was something in her personality, or aura, or whatever one called it, that reached out and caressed his heart. He realized he wasn't as sad, or mad, when she was around. Truth be told, he kinda liked who he was in her presence.

"Alright, you two lovebirds, time to say goodnight," Skeeter called out, then laughed.

Well, he liked who he was in her presence when Skeeter *wasn't* around. At that moment, he wanted nothing more than to hogtie the boy and teach him a lesson or two. "Sorry about that. I don't think Skeeter mentally developed past the age of twelve."

"It's alright. He's just teasing. It's his way of showing he cares about you."

"Pft, yeah, right." And Sam had a bridge he'd like to sell her if she actually believed that hogwash.

Nelly giggled. "Well, maybe not. But I do need to get back home and check on the dogs. Let them out to run before putting them all to bed." She started to walk off the porch and turned around.

The look in her eyes was enough to make him want more. But that couldn't be. Once she found out the truth about him, those looks would turn to pity. And he didn't want that. Just the idea of her pitying him ruined the good mood he had going. So, he waved without smiling when she fluttered her fingers toward him before getting in her truck.

If only Afghanistan hadn't ended the way it did.

$$Chapter\ 9$$

Nelly smiled the entire way home. Not only was dinner tasty, but the company wasn't bad, either. Well, maybe a couple of the men could be better behaved, but it was to be expected when they all lived together and there weren't many women around. It didn't seem like any of them had girlfriends. Maybe she should play matchmaker for a few of the guys? A good woman usually helped immature men to grow up and act their age.

Sadly, she didn't really know anyone yet. The only women she'd really spoken to so far were either married or engaged. "Huh, am I the last single woman in town?" She shook her head at that thought. Nelly just needed to get out and meet more people, specifically more women.

And that was exactly what she planned for Sunday morning. Church services were usually full of single women and families. This Sunday she'd be attending the local Christian church. But until then, she needed to focus on getting the house taken care of.

First thing Friday morning, Nelly called the waste management number. They were more than happy to set up a Monday morning delivery of their largest dumpster and have it swapped out on Friday for another one. Now that she had her one big assignment for the day done, she could focus on her dogs.

Before she made her call, Nelly had put the dogs out in the paddock. It was a beautiful late May day. The sun had come up and was warming the dirt and the flowers. A rich perfume scented the air as the sun climbed higher and higher in the sky. Nelly took in a deep breath and knew she was home. In the old garden, the sweet peas had bloomed and their rich scent of orange blossom and honey filled the air.

When she inhaled again, she picked up notes of lavender. She'd have to pick some and dry them out. Sachets of lavender would be good for the house once it was all cleared out. Maybe she'd add some of the sweet peas, too. An added benefit to the property was the flower garden. Sure, it needed a lot of work, but some of those perennials just couldn't be stopped.

If she was lucky, there might even be a few vegetables in the garden. Or better yet, some herbs she could use in her cooking once she had a proper stove. Which reminded her, she needed to call Sam.

"Sam, hi."

Sam interrupted her before she could let him know why she'd called. "Nelly, good morning. Sorry I haven't had a chance to get ahold of the Department of Wildlife."

"No worries, Sam. I've already set up the dumpster to arrive Monday morning. But what I really wanted to know about was the stove." Nelly cringed as she waited to hear if Sam had asked about a loaner for her.

The sound of laughter in the background caught Nelly's attention, and she strained to hear what they were saying. It must have been more ribbing, because she could tell Sam was walking away from them; their sounds were getting softer and more distant.

"Sorry, I should have sent it home with you last night. I do have a camp stove and a barbecue you can use. When Jerod gets back, I'm sure he'll have an actual stove somewhere you can use until your house is ready."

"Thanks. Should I come by and pick it up?" Until the dumpster arrived and they cleared out some of the rooms in the house, Nelly didn't have much to do. If she were to get the gear Sam was offering to loan her, she could start making fresh meals for herself and maybe even start making some candles, too.

"No, no. Don't worry about coming here. I need to head into town, so I'll drop by with the stove and grill. Say, in about an hour?" Sam sounded unsure, and his voice quavered just a bit—not quite a question, but also not a direct statement.

Nelly held in her laugh. She knew why he wanted to come to her instead of the other way around. And truth be told, she couldn't blame him. The guys had done their darndest to embarrass them both last night at dinner. She wasn't up for a repeat, either. "Sure, sounds good. Should I have a pot of tea or coffee on for you when you arrive?"

"Coffee'd be great. Thanks." Sam hung up.

Nelly smiled and stuffed her phone into her back pocket. Then she called out to the dogs: "Hier." She named each one to ensure they all showed up. They knew their names and were extraordinarily obedient whenever she used the German commands.

Although, today it seemed like the dogs took a bit longer than usual to obey. Nelly was walking out of the barn to see where they were when they came running toward her. All four stopped quickly in front of her. She looked behind them to see what they might have been up to, but could only see the overgrown grass and a few pink flowers that had grown next to the fence.

For the next thirty minutes she took the dogs through their paces, practicing each command to ensure they never forgot. Thankfully, she had set an alarm on her phone to remind her to clean up and set the coffee pot.

When she packed to move, she included a standard Mr. Coffee pot, an electric kettle, and a French press. When it was just her drinking coffee she preferred the French press, even though she had read the articles boo-hooing them. The diterpenes from the unfiltered beans tended to raise cholesterol levels and had been linked to heart disease. But since she didn't do more than a few cups a week in the press, she figured she'd be fine.

The problem was filtered coffee just didn't have the same flavor and aroma as a French press. Some might say she was a bit of a coffee snob, but she had been to Seattle and met plenty of true coffee snobs. She wasn't even in their league. Nelly just knew good coffee when she tasted it.

The coffee was brewing, and the aroma was unbelievable. Earlier in the week she had gone into town and visited the Frenchtown Roasting Company, where she picked up a coffee and cinnamon roll. But she also picked up a couple pounds of the latest brew Lottie had going that day.

An aroma of rich, deep notes filled her senses, and she relaxed as she let the lightly caramelized scent enter her body and fill her with sweet memories of sitting on her parents' porch and drinking coffee on lazy Saturdays with her family.

"Hi, is this the right place?" a deep voice with a hint of laughter called out.

Nelly realized she had her eyes closed and a lazy smile on her face as she looked heavenward. She turned to look at her guest. "I guess it depends on where you're supposed to be."

"I thought I was heading to a nightmare house, but it smells like I ended up in nirvana." Sam grinned and walked into the barn.

All four dogs raised their heads from the relaxed positions they had been in and gave Sam a once-over. None of them seemed worried; in fact, Rogue went over to him and nudged the man's legs.

"Hey there, buddy." Sam leaned over and used his right hand to scratch between the boxer's eyes.

Rogue's tongue lolled to the side and his stub of a tail wagged back and forth with his backside. It seemed the dog had taken a liking to Sam, and if Nelly wasn't mistaken, the feeling was mutual.

"I think Rogue likes you." Nelly tilted her head and watched the pair.

Sam chuckled. "Unlike Spike."

Speaking of which. The unruly dog didn't exactly growl at Sam, but he did show his teeth. Almost as though Spike was claiming his territory, the dog bumped up next to Nelly and took a defensive stance.

Nelly was about to get after Spike, but since the dog hadn't done anything bad yet, she held off. "Well, I think Spike has an issue with most men, so don't feel bad."

"I won't." Sam continued to rub Rogue's head. Once he stopped, the dog sat at his feet and looked up longingly at the veteran-turned-cowboy.

"How about a cup of coffee?" Nelly offered.

"Sure, cream and sugar?"

"Coming right up. Take a seat anywhere you like." Nelly went to the little kitchenette where she had the coffee maker and set about getting their cups made.

When she came out, she almost dropped the mugs in her hands. Sam had sat down in a chair, but what caught her attention was the fact that not only Rogue had sat at his feet, but so did Buffy. Rogue had his head in Sam's lap while Buffy laid her head on Sam's feet. If her hands hadn't been full, she'd have taken out her cell phone and snapped a picture.

"Hey, now. Don't you go getting any ideas about stealing my dogs from me." Nelly handed Sam his mug of coffee.

The cowboy grinned. "Thanks. If the dogs somehow up and disappear in the middle of the night, it won't be me that's taken them."

She arched a brow. "Oh, really?"

"Nope. It will most likely be that death trap of a house that's sucked them up inside." Sam's eyes sparkled with mischief as he took another sip of his coffee. "Mm, this must be Lottie's latest brew?"

"Yes, it is. Now don't go changing the subject here." She took her seat only a couple feet away from Sam and relaxed back into the camp chair she'd been using ever since she arrived. It had a desert camo design with the Army's logo on the back of her chair. Her brother had brought it back from boot camp. She loved it and always felt as though he was right there with her when she used it.

"But, this coffee is so good. How can I *not* want to talk about it?" He took another sip. "And drink it."

"Uh-huh. Now just what did you mean about the house swallowing up my dogs?" Nelly watched Sam as he moved in his chair. The man had on a tight-fitting pair of denim jeans, a blue-and-white checked, long-sleeve cowboy shirt, and a brown pair of boots with an intricate blue design on the sides. He looked as though he'd grown up on a ranch and never left.

Before they could continue their banter, another truck pulled up right outside the barn. All four dogs stood at attention. Rogue stayed next to Sam, but the other three surrounded Nelly as though they were her personal security force and an unknown enemy was approaching.

When an unknown man walked into the barn with a huge smile on his face, Spike growled.

"Fuss," Nelly commanded, telling Spike to heel.

Sam stood and furrowed his brows. "Jerod, we weren't expecting you until tomorrow night."

Jerod, wearing jeans, brown boots, and a short-sleeved, button-up cowboy shirt, walked in and shook Sam's hand. "Nice to see you, too."

Nelly had never met Jerod in person; they'd only spoken over the phone or messaged via email. She wasn't sure what she had expected, but it wasn't a handsome cowboy who smiled from ear to ear. At times when they spoke he had come off as gruff, similar to how Sam was when she first met him.

"What I meant was, I thought you were on your honeymoon. Is everything alright?" Sam hadn't moved, other than to stand when he shook Jerod's hand. Partly because Rogue blocked his legs. The boxer seemed to be protecting Sam, not unlike the other three dogs were doing for Nelly.

It was good. She had trained them to be protective of their handlers. But Sam wasn't a handler, and she doubted he was even in line for a service dog. The man seemed to be doing very well, other than being rough around the edges when others were teasing him. But that was to be expected.

"Well, are you going to introduce me?" Jerod grinned at Nelly and waited.

"Oh, right." Sam cleared his throat.

Nelly wanted to know what had brought him back early from his honeymoon as well, but the introductions were more important at the moment.

"Nelly, this here is Jerod Stevens, owner of the Crooked Arrow Ranch." Sam motioned to Jerod, then turned back to Nelly. "And this is Nelly Wilson, owner of this here, uh, ranch?"

A nervous laughed escaped Nelly and she coughed to try and cover it. "Hi. Nice to finally meet you, Jerod."

"You as well. And I'm so sorry I wasn't here when you arrived. I thought you weren't coming in until Monday?" Jerod put his hand out, and Nelly shook it.

"I wasn't, but I found myself eager to get going, and it's a good thing I did, too."

"Oh." Jerod's eyes narrowed. "Why's that?"

"Have you seen my house?" Nelly snorted and shook her head.

The newcomer turned around and winced as he looked at the main ranch house. "Yeah, I had hoped to be here when you arrived so I could help you. I take it your Realtor failed to tell you about the condition of the house?"

"Yup, and when I confronted him, he basically said 'caveat emptor.'" Nelly snarled when she thought of the schemer.

"Well, I hope the barn has been a safe and clean place for you." Jerod looked around and nodded his approval.

"Were you the one who cleaned it all up?" Nelly looked from Jerod to Sam, who smirked. It felt like he was saying, *"I told you so,"* with his eyes.

"Actually, I had one of the town boys take care of it. I was too busy planning my wedding."

"Yes, I heard about it. It sounded really nice. And congratulations." She looked behind Jerod, expecting to see his new bride, but no one was there.

Realizing what she was doing, Jerod said, "she's back at the ranch getting unpacked. We just arrived home when Mike told me about you being here all week. I'm really sorry I couldn't have helped more. But I'm here now and happy to do whatever I can to make sure you get the house in order." The smile left his face, and while he still had the happy gleam of a newlywed shining in his eyes, his lips turned down when he looked back at the house again.

"No worries, boss. We've got it all under control. Monday morning a dumpster will arrive, and I've already put together a team of men to help clean it out." Sam went on to tell Jerod more details about what they had planned, and who was assigned to junk the house.

Jerod and Nelly discussed payment details, and he told her the same thing Sam had. "You can wait until you get a grant coming through. These guys needed a new assignment anyways."

"Please tell me my house isn't what brought you back early?" If word had gotten back to Jerod while he was on his honeymoon, and he had come home early for her, she was going to feel like a heel.

The newlywed shook his head. "No, that's not why." He lowered his voice. "We actually planned to come back a day early. We wanted to have a day of rest at home so we could be fresh for Monday morning."

Sam raised his eyebrows. "Really? Why didn't you tell anyone?" He fisted his right hand at his side.

Nelly noticed and hoped Sam wasn't feeling as though Jerod didn't trust him. She didn't quite understand their relationship, or why Sam was even still at the ranch. He seemed like a man who was ready to get a job and reintegrate with society. Wasn't that the goal of the ranch—heal up, learn a new trade, get a job, and get back out there?

"Well, we had hoped to slip inside the house unnoticed and spend some time alone." Pink worked its way up Jerod's cheeks, which made him look like a sweet, innocent teenager instead of the thirty-something cowboy and ranch owner he was.

Sam guffawed and opened his mouth to say something, but the look coming from Jerod at that moment quieted him.

"Well, I'm sorry you had to come all the way out here, basically for nothing. Why don't you call me next week when you're back on schedule and we can set up a time to meet and discuss... I mean, uh, give me a call when call you're ready." Nelly wasn't quite sure what all Jerod had told Sam about her job there, and she didn't want to be the one to spill the beans.

"What are you talking about?" Sam narrowed his eyes and looked at Jerod.

Jerod quirked his mouth and paused for a moment. "Well, I was going to tell everyone Sunday night after supper." He looked to Nelly.

"Nelly here's a dog trainer. She has a program for service dogs."

"Yeah, I know," Sam interrupted. "But what does that have to do with the Crooked Arrow?"

After a deep sigh, a wariness crossed Jerod's face, and Nelly wondered why he was so hesitant to say anything. "The Crooked Arrow is partnering with Nelly. We're going to pair up a wounded vet with a service dog where needed."

"It's a program specifically developed to help returning war veterans deal with PTSD, and the resulting issues that can accompany the disorder." Nelly had said this line so many times when she interviewed for government grants that she could repeat it in her sleep, and she probably did when she dreamt about the program and her dogs.

Sam didn't look too happy. "Why didn't you tell me? Am I on the list of disabled bodies who needs a babysitter?"

Nelly's head jerked back. "What are you talking about? I don't make the call, and besides, from what I've seen you don't need a service dog. That's up to Jerod and Megan. I only work with the patient and the dog once they're paired up."

"Right, like you don't know about this..." He held up his prosthetic arm for all to see. It was still covered with his glove and the long sleeve, but when he moved his arm up high enough, part of the plastic arm was visible. While the doctors had done a good job of matching the color of his skin tone to the plastic, it still didn't look like a real arm.

Surprise passed over Nelly's face. Before she realized what she had done, her eyes bugged out and she was speechless. She knew he had an issue with his left arm, but she'd had no clue what the issue was. "I...um... Sorry." She ran a hand over her face and then stood up tall and tried to remove all emotion. "I had no idea what brought you to the ranch."

She felt like a fool. What did one say to someone who'd lost their arm serving their country? *Hey, sorry you lost your arm, but no worries, here's a dog for you.* Yeah, right. That would never work. And to make matters worse, she could see the anger boiling up in his eyes. And she deserved it, too. He wasn't the first injured soldier she'd come across, and he wouldn't be the last. She knew better than to feel pity, and especially knew *not* to show it. Unfortunately, she could feel the emotion on her face the moment she realized what she was looking at.

Her pity hurt him, and she knew it.

# Chapter 10

Without a word, Sam stormed out of the barn, not bothering to look back. He didn't even say goodbye to Rogue. He may not have been a whole man, but he was still a man, and not a child. Sam Marley didn't need any stinkin' dog keeping an eye on him. He could do just fine on his own, thank you very much.

"Where does she get off deciding that I need a dog and not even talking to me about it?" He was fuming as he got into his truck and started the engine. The entire way back to the ranch, he steamed and grumbled. "I knew I should never have gotten so close to a pretty woman. They're nothing but trouble."

Once he was home, he slammed the front door shut and headed to his room.

Behind him, he could hear Skeeter's grating voice. "Geesh, looks like someone's back to his old grumpy self."

When Sam slammed his bedroom door closed, he shut out the rest of the world.

"She looked at me with such pity. I knew this would happen. Why didn't I listen to my own advice?" Sam took off his shirt, then unhooked the prosthetic arm. He'd been fitted with it over three years earlier, and it didn't chafe as much as it once did, but he still needed a break from the end of the device and his stub.

At least it wasn't winter. When it was extra cold and the wind howled, his arm dried out and he had to take off the prosthetic device and apply a special cream to help moisturize his skin, to keep the chafing away. Now that it was summer, he didn't need to do it as often.

Once the cream was rubbed into his skin, he sat on the edge of his bed, shirtless and feeling sorry for himself. It was times like these that he wished he'd never left the sandpit.

At least not alive.

He thought back to the last fight with the insurgents and fell back on his bed, breathing hard. Sweat began to form at his temples and he closed his eyes to the horror he remembered. In his mind, he'd gone back in time by over three years. His friend Henry was there, next to him beside the Humvee.

They were about the same age and had joined only one month apart. While they had attended different basic training and advanced training, they met each other when they were both assigned to the 75th Infantry in Fort Lewis, Washington. Over the next few years they had been reassigned to different bases, but eventually both found their way back to Fort Lewis and were now Rangers and assigned to the 2nd Battalion. They had only been in Washington State for a few months before they had been deployed to support the Global War on Terrorism.

While serving together in Afghanistan, they became close friends. And when they were attacked while making their way to a mountain where the enemy had embedded themselves, they stuck to each other like glue. A roadside bomb had hit their Humvee and it was laying on its side, smoking and now useless.

The enemy was all around trying to get close enough to either kill the survivors, or worse.

Sam remembered their conversation that day. "Henry, I'm almost out of ammo. What you got?" He wasn't sure if it was what the military had once called "shell shock" or if his friend had hurt himself, but Henry didn't answer. Sam knew he was physically alright. There was some blood, and the sergeant was covered in dirt and debris from the bombing of their Humvee, but Sam was the one who had difficulty moving his left arm. "Henry? You alright, man?"

"Huh? Oh, yeah. Sorry." Henry shook his head and put his fingers in his ears as though he was trying to clear water out after a long day in the lake. "Can't hear too well." As evidenced by his loud voice.

"Shh. They'll hear you." Sam turned to look into his friend's eyes and put a finger to his lips.

With a hand to one of his ears, Henry looked at Sam confused, and then when his hearing began to clear up, he heard footsteps.

What happened next was still a bit fuzzy. Sam knew there was a fight, several shots fired, and a knife embedded in his elbow. But when the smoke cleared, he and Henry were still alive, if barely, while the enemy wasn't. That was all that mattered at the time. Now, he wasn't so sure those terrorists didn't have it better.

Sure, they weren't where they had been told they'd end up. There was no way anyone who committed such atrocities against humanity would end up in paradise with ten virgins. That was what their terrorist leaders had told them would happen if they died while fighting the *unclean Westerners*. No, Sam knew where they were—hell. They deserved it, too.

But if Sam's Sunday school teacher was right, if he'd have died that day he would be in heaven with God. No more pain, and no more guilt. And not just guilt over killing men in war, but guilt over letting his men down in Afghanistan, and when they returned. Since that day, he couldn't bring himself to pray anymore. He no longer read his Bible, and forget about attending church.

Before Sam could spiral any deeper in his shame and guilt, he heard a knock at his door. He brought himself back to the present and sat up. He wasn't in the mood for any company. The last thing he needed was someone making him feel even more guilt, and even lesser of a man for slamming doors and hiding away.

Another knock came, this time with a melodic voice. "Sam? It's me, Megan. Can I come in?"

A few cuss words escaped his lips, but thankfully under his breath. One of the things Jerod stressed was cleaning up one's mouth. If you couldn't use words fit for a kid's ears, then they weren't worth saying. That was part of why he'd stayed quiet for so long when he first arrived. And also because his Nana would slap him upside his head if she could hear the words tumbling about in his head.

Thankfully, he had learned at a very young age to keep those words out of his mouth when Nana was around. It only took one slap up the back of his head and two mouth washings with Lava soap to learn to keep his bad mouth shut. Of course, the slaps of an old grandma never hurt. When he laughed, she learned quickly. Which was why she switched to washing his mouth out with the most disgusting soap this side of the Atlantic.

He missed his Nana. She'd get him if she were still alive. She'd probably be the only one who did.

Another knock and another question. "Sam, I'm here to talk or to listen, whichever you prefer. No judging, you know that."

And he did know that. Megan had been his lifeline since coming to the Crooked Arrow Ranch. She had been the only one since he'd lost his arm who didn't pity him. And she was a good listener.

For two seconds he thought about asking her out when he left the ranch, but then remembered his promise to never get involved again. Something he'd forgotten this past week.

With a heavy sigh, he stood and opened the door. "Come on in." Sam stood back and waved for her to enter.

Megan stood in the doorway, scowling. "How about you put your arm and shirt back on, then meet me in my office?"

After a few heartbeats, he looked down and realized what he'd done. He'd never answered the door to anyone, not even a male doctor, without at least a shirt on to cover his stub and scars. The stub, just above where an elbow should be, wasn't the only evidence of his battle wounds. His left side, abdomen, and back were covered in scars from the shrapnel he'd taken after the roadside bomb went off.

"Ah, right. Sorry about that." Sam instinctively tried to move his left arm to cover his chest, then remembered too late his arm was gone. He felt heat radiating up his chest and into his neck and face.

Cool as a cucumber, Megan turned and waved over her head. "Five minutes. And I want to see you in my office."

Sam closed the door and sat back down on the bed, releasing a breath he didn't realize he'd been holding. He cleared his mind of all thoughts about his friend, and what happened once they were back in the states, and put himself back together. The nursery rhyme "Humpty Dumpty" ran through his mind on repeat until he found himself in Megan's office.

She looked up from the notebook she was writing in and motioned for him to take a seat. "Do you want to talk?"

Of course he didn't want to talk about what had happened. But it was a requirement to stay there. And Sam hadn't felt this comfortable anywhere since he joined the US Army Rangers, 2nd Battalion in Washington State. Not even his mother had made him feel so welcome as Megan did since the war.

Probably because his mother had cried so many times when he came home from Afghanistan.

Staying away from home wasn't just for his benefit, it was for his family, too. They deserved better than him for a son, a brother, and a friend. He kept in touch with letters and calls, but since arriving at the Crooked Arrow, he'd not been home.

Knowing he had to say something, Sam looked up at Megan. "She found out, and the pity in her eyes almost destroyed me." He ran a hand through his hair and looked back down at his feet. "I thought about that day. The one that changed everything."

The two of them spent more than the normal hour discussing what had happened and how it made Sam feel. He almost didn't tell Megan how much he wished he hadn't come home at all, but he knew if he didn't, the thoughts would fester and boil in his soul. He'd come a long way the past year, and he didn't want to go back to the nightmare that was his world before he met Megan. They were even weaning him off his anti-depressants—something he really wanted to do. If he let himself fall into a bottomless pit of despair, he'd be back on those meds at full prescription.

While he had no issue with anyone taking those types of meds when they needed to, he knew he could get off them if he worked really hard. He was a US Army Ranger, for fig's sake. He could do anything he set his mind to. And he'd set his mind to getting off those drugs that only made him numb.

After Sam unburdened himself, he sat back exhausted and wiped the sweat from his brow.

Usually, Megan said something. But today she sat there staring at him with a question in her eyes.

"What?" he asked.

She sighed, then leaned forward and put her arms on her desk. "Sam, how would you feel about having a dog?"

"Pftt," Sam scoffed. "Was this the plan the whole time? Bring that lady here and ambush me with a babysitter?" Anger was starting to seep into his soul once again. This was too much. He stood up to leave.

Megan put a hand up to stop him from leaving. "Wait. You're not being fair."

He crossed his arms over his chest and glared at Megan. "I thought you were on my side?"

"I am. Which is why I just now thought about it." Megan pursed her lips. He knew she was getting frustrated when she jerked back in her chair and shook her head. "Sam, I hadn't planned on getting you a service dog. Neither had Jerod."

"Then what is *she* doing here?" A pain ratcheted through Sam's chest as he thought about Nelly. She was supposed to be his friend, not his... Well, he didn't know what she'd be if she paired him with a dog. Would she be his trainer? Like he was a dog needing to be told how to act.

Megan sighed and took in a deep breath before releasing it. "Sam, it's true she's here to train her dogs. Jerod offered her a chance to work with our veterans..."

Sam interrupted. "I thought you said it wasn't planned?"

"Wait just a second. Let me explain." An exasperated Megan took a drink of her water. "The plan was for Nelly and her dogs to train with our veterans, who volunteered, and to help her dogs finish their training. She's new to training service dogs for vets. We were all going to work together. And if a few of our own veterans ended up with service dogs, then even better. But there was never a plan to pair our vets with a dog permanently. And it will only happen when the veteran and the dog gel. This can't be forced—you'll have to want it."

"And what if I don't?" Sam turned defiant eyes on his counselor.

"Then you won't be paired. It's just"—she sat back again in her chair—"I think a companion would be good for you. You don't seem to trust people very much, and a dog could help you. He'll love you unconditionally. And he'll look out for you. No one will ever be as dedicated to you as a dog." She tilted her head. "Scratch that, after God, no one will ever be as dedicated to you as a dog."

Sam snorted. "Right, God and dogs. Sure, that's what's going to help me get my head screwed back on straight."

They both sat there looking at each other. Sam glared while Megan looked thoughtful.

"Well, it won't work unless you want it to. But I will pray for you. Will you pray?" Megan hadn't brought God into the sessions with Sam very often. When she did, he usually shut down, even though she knew he'd grown up attending services.

This time when pain shot through his chest, Sam winced. For so long he'd been angry with God. Why did God allow war? Why did so many good people have to die? Why did God save him, but not his buddy, Henry? Why did He let Henry kill himself? And why in the world did he feel so guilty about Henry's death?

All Sam wanted was for the pain to go away.

"Maybe," Sam whispered, not wanting Megan to hear him. Or at least he didn't want her to expect him to go to church.

*Chapter 11*

The rest of the day, Nelly felt listless and just plain awful. She knew better than anyone that you never, *ever* showed pity to someone who'd been injured in war. After her brother came home, she'd gone through some training to help him, but it wasn't enough. Then when she changed her focus from people who dealt with physical disabilities to those who suffered from PTSD and sometimes also had to deal with a physical disability, she learned even more about how to treat patients like Sam, and her brother.

A person suffering from PTSD had so many more issues than just bad memories or nightmares. They could have waking nightmares that felt real while they were up and walking around. And a plethora of other symptoms. Even the experts couldn't agree on all of the symptoms that represented PTSD.

Nelly had once Googled the symptoms of PTSD. Of course, too many pages to count came up. But even the top pages showed three main symptoms on one site. Another listed seventeen, and still another listed five. Everyone reacted with varying levels of the most common symptoms, too.

And the worst was the guilt. Almost every single PTSD patient Nelly had heard about suffered from survivor's guilt at the very least, and some even dealt with guilt over what they had to do on the battlefield.

Her father had a friend who had served in Vietnam. He was a helicopter pilot. The man went through life without letting on what he suffered from. Then one day he cleaned all of his clothes, set his apartment to rights, and took off in his car. He was found two days later at the bottom of a ravine with a note in his pocket.

It wasn't an accident.

Turned out, his unit was ordered to open fire on a village full of Viet Cong fighters. Only their intel was wrong. Most of the unit never even made it home, and those that did suffered from PTSD. The issues were compounded because the US government and the VA doctors hadn't recognized PTSD until recently.

And even now they still didn't always know how best to handle each patient.

Nelly couldn't believe how brave Sam was. He'd never let on that he had lost his left arm. While she didn't know the whole story—Jerod told her it was Sam's story to tell—he did tell her that Sam had been doing better and better as the past year had progressed.

Her stupid reaction had probably set Sam back in his treatment and healing. Before Jerod left, they talked about Sam and how best to help him.

"Jerod, I'm so sorry. I had no idea. I mean..." Nelly was messing everything up, and she plopped down on the chair. "I did know something was wrong with his left arm. He always wore long sleeves and a glove on that one hand. I actually thought he had been in a fire and his hand and arm were burned so badly that he didn't want anyone to see."

Jerod put up a hand. "Please, don't stress over it. This is part of the healing process. Out on the ranch we're all in such a bubble. Even when we go into town we're pretty insulated. Most of the residents of Frenchtown know we're all wounded veterans, but they accept everyone as they are."

"And I show up, and what do I do?" She threw her hands in the air. "And I know better."

"Nelly, you couldn't have known what Sam was going through. But I should warn you, he's not the only one with a prosthetic. When you come to the ranch you're going to meet men, and eventually women, who have prosthetics that you can see, and some you may not see. Please remember that, and your training."

They had made plans to meet up after church the next day, and Nelly was looking forward to meeting Dana. The men at the ranch had spoken very highly of her, as did the barista Nelly saw every time she went into town for coffee and a roll.

After Jerod left, Nelly thought back to the disabled people she'd worked with so far. Most of them were blind or deaf. She did have one woman who was in a wheelchair. When she'd met each of them for the first time she hadn't reacted poorly to them, or their disability.

So why did Sam's prosthetic arm affect her so much?

After a fitful night of sleep, Nelly arose early and worked with the dogs before she went to church. As she drove to the local Christian church, she prayed that God would soothe her aching heart, and also help Sam to heal. She was going to have to ask his forgiveness the next time she saw him, if he'd even talk to her again.

The pastor's voice soothed her aching soul, but more importantly, the message spoke to her heart and head. She didn't know how he did it, but somehow the pastor knew exactly what she needed to hear.

*Humble yourselves therefore under the mighty hand of God, that he may exalt you in due time: Casting all your care upon him; for he careth for you. Be sober, be vigilant; because your adversary the devil, as a roaring lion, walketh about, seeking whom he may devour: Whom resist stedfast in the faith, knowing that the same afflictions are accomplished in your brethren that are in the world. But the God of all grace, who hath called us unto his eternal glory by Christ Jesus, after that ye have suffered a while, make you perfect, stablish, strengthen, settle you. – 1 Peter 6 – 10 KJV.*

"Brothers and sisters, Peter is giving us hope. He told us two thousand years ago that God is here for us. He wants to take our burdens away." The pastor paused and looked directly at Nelly, and his lips turned up just enough to tell her that he knew she needed this message.

"God doesn't want you to stress about the cares of this world. He also doesn't want you to feel guilty about anything you've done, or think you've done. The key to joy is giving your cares over to God. Let him bear the pain. It's the devil who wants you to worry and feel guilty. That guilt can cause a rift between you and God, and that's exactly what the enemy wants." He hit the pulpit as he stressed the last sentence.

"Don't let the enemy win. Go to God." The pastor looked around and paused when he saw someone in the audience. It was a long enough pause that Nelly looked around to see who he was looking at.

Nelly gasped when she saw him. Sam had come. She wasn't sure she'd get a chance to see him any time soon after yesterday. Would he forgive her?

"Ever hear the phrase, 'Let go... Let God?' It's based on this passage in 1 Peter. When you let go of everything holding you back from living a life of joy, and let God take over, then life truly begins for the believer. Joy has a chance to permeate your entire being, and the cares of this world melt away. The pain you're feeling from difficult circumstances in your past goes away, only to be replaced by contentment." The pastor continued to look at Sam, and when he looked away she noticed him glance her way before settling his gaze on someone else in the audience she didn't know.

As the service continued, Nelly's heart lightened. At the end of the service, she sat in her pew and prayed to the Lord and gave her guilt over Sam to God. When she finally stood up to leave, it felt as though she'd released a ton of bricks from her shoulders. She still had some guilt she was holding tightly, but this one she decided to let go and let God.

The moment Nelly walked outside, she took a deep breath of the sun-filled air and sighed. The sun was high in the sky and a few wispy clouds floated overhead. The green leafy trees nearby looked as they were lightly waving a hello to her in tune to the breeze. It was a warm day, but not too hot. She couldn't have asked for a better Sunday afternoon.

Out of the corner of her eye, she caught Jerod's attention as he waved to her. Next to him was a beautiful auburn-haired woman who smiled from ear to ear. They made their way to her as Nelly walked toward them.

"Nelly, good to see you today." Jerod put a hand out.

Nelly shook his hand and grinned. "Jerod, it's good to see you, too. Is this your wife?"

When Jerod took his hand back, he put it around his wife's shoulders and pulled her close. "Yes, this is my Dana." Then he looked back to Nelly. "Dana, this is Nelly. She's the new dog trainer in town."

Green eyes sparkled when Dana smiled. "So nice to meet you. I've heard a lot about you."

"All good, I hope." A shiver of nerves rolled through Nelly as she prayed that Sam wasn't saying anything bad about her. Although, she doubted he'd be going around and badmouthing her. Or at least, she hoped he wouldn't.

"Very good." Dana grinned at her husband. "My husband here's been talking about you for a while now. I'm so glad you made it here safely." She chuckled. "And gladder that you've got a dumpster coming to the house tomorrow." A visible shiver went down her entire body.

Nelly chuckled. "Yeah, that seems to be the general sentiment. Turns out everyone but me knew how scary that house was."

"I'm sorry Lank didn't tell you about it. Had I known he didn't disclose the true shape, I would have had Jerod tell you." Dana seemed to be a genuinely sweet woman. Nelly was looking forward to getting to know the newlywed.

Considering the fact that she'd be spending a lot of time at the Crooked Arrow, she was confident she'd get plenty of chances to make this woman one of her new friends. Plus, if she continued to work at the local coffee shop, then they would most certainly see a lot of each other.

"Do you have supper plans today? We've got a roast in the crock pot back at the ranch, and I'd love to have you join us." Dana's hopeful expression caused Nelly to stop and think.

One the one hand, a homemade roast would be wonderful, and she'd get a chance to get to know more of the guys at the ranch. But on the other hand was Sam. Would he be upset if she came over so soon?

Dana must have noticed her indecision, for she looked around, then whispered, "Don't worry about Sam. He's a curmudgeonly ol' coot, but down deep he's actually a nice man. He'll come around."

The thought that Dana already knew about the fight set Nelly on edge.

"Come on. You really should join us today," Jerod encouraged.

Not knowing how to say no to these two, Nelly agreed. "Alright. And thank you. It's been a while since I've had a roast. And from the looks of things, it's going to be a long time before I can cook anything halfway decent at home."

They all laughed.

"Actually, we might have a solution for you. Just until you can get your house in some semblance of a living condition."

Jerod's cryptic response had Nelly's attention.

"Oh really? How's that?" Nelly asked.

"Come to lunch and I'll tell you."

He was one tricky cowboy.

Chapter 12

He couldn't believe it when he saw her enter the front door. It was one thing to know she was at his church that morning, but quite another to have her in his safe place. Sam still wasn't sure what he thought about Megan's offer of getting a service dog, but he was sure he was still mad at Nelly for not telling him the truth.

Instead of hanging around, Sam turned to head back to his room.

"Sam, why don't you come join us." Jerod's words weren't a request; they were an order.

And the one thing Sam still did without thought was obey commands from his superiors. Didn't matter that he was no longer in the Army, or that he'd been out for three years now. The chain of command had been instilled in him during his entire time in service. That would be one of those habits he probably wouldn't break any time soon.

Not wanting to show any weakness, Sam straightened his shoulders and turned around. He couldn't help the frown permanently etched on his face, but surely nobody would expect him to smile.

"Nelly, hello." The formal greeting came out sounding a bit monotone to Sam, but he thought it was good enough.

"Hi Sam." At least Nelly wasn't trying to talk to him. Maybe the day could be salvaged if she kept away from him.

Nelly's smile faltered when he turned away and headed toward the dining room. He heard her offering to help Dana with lunch and his shoulders drooped. She was staying? He should have known she was invited to lunch after church. They always brought people over for lunch after Sunday services.

Sam grabbed a seat next to Mike and nodded to the quiet man. He was always a good person to sit next to at the dinner table, for he rarely chatted. And when he did say something it was usually a question about what they were going to do for work either later that day or the next. And those sorts of questions never bothered Sam.

"Mike." Sam took his napkin and placed it on his lap.

"Sam. Is everything ready for tomorrow at the new Wilson ranch?" Mike took a sip of his water.

"Wilson ranch?" Sam wasn't sure what Mike was talking about. The only assignment they'd had for the week, outside of their regular Crooked Arrow chores, was... Then it dawned on him. Mike was calling the old Brown ranch the Wilson ranch now that Nelly owned it. It would take some getting used to, but he'd eventually think of that place as hers.

Before Sam could say anything, Nelly entered the dining room with a large bowl of salad. She set it on the other end of the table, farthest from him. Sam prayed she'd sit at that end, too. He'd purposely taken a seat closer to Jerod thinking that Nelly would sit closer to Dana, who always sat at the foot of the table.

He held his breath when Nelly stood up and left the room. She must have been getting more food to put on the table. Even though he was still ticked off with her, he couldn't help but wish her back to the table. Which was stupid, of course. He needed her away from him. She represented his weakness, and he couldn't have that.

"Well?" Mike asked.

"Well, what?" Sam responded. "Oh, you mean tomorrow?"

Mike nodded and looked heavenward like a teenager exasperated with his clueless parent.

Frowning, Sam opened his mouth to say something when he noticed Jerod enter and take his regular seat at the head of the table, right next to him.

"So, Sam. What did you think about today's sermon?" Usually Jerod smiled when talking about church, but today he had a thoughtful look on his face.

"Um, it was good." Brevity was going to be Sam's motto for the afternoon. He was having a tough time thinking about anything other than the pretty dog trainer. Wait, he couldn't think about her unless it was to cuss her out. No, that wasn't fair, either. His Nana had raised him better than that. While he wouldn't cuss her out, even in his head, he didn't have to talk to her. Or think about her.

"That's it? It's good?" Jerod shook his head and furrowed his brow.

"What do you want me to say? That all my troubles are over now? I've given everything to God and no longer feel guilty for getting my entire squad killed?" Sam pushed his chair back and left the table.

Everyone in the dining room stopped talking and looked at him. Sam was used to being stared at, but not by this lot. Normally they ignored him unless they needed something. A feeling of unease spread throughout his body and he headed to his room, stomach rumbling.

The last thing on his mind was eating.

## Chapter 13

Nelly had just opened the door to the dining room with a plate of roasted potatoes when she heard the last of Sam's tirade. She watched helplessly as he stormed out of the room. After she placed the platter on the table she bit her lip, then asked the group, "Is this because of me?"

She knew he wasn't happy she was there. It was just as Nelly feared, and he was still mad as spit at her. Maybe she should have said something about what she was doing with Jerod, but she didn't want to speak out of turn. It was Jerod and Megan who were going to choose which veterans received a service dog and which ones would work with her on training the dogs.

Even though Sam had seemed so normal, and so well adjusted when she first arrived, it just went to show that you really didn't know someone that well until adversity struck. Nelly wouldn't have imagined his response, not in a million years. It wasn't like she was coming to take his arm away. She was just in town to work with some of the residents of the Crooked Arrow Ranch. Although, looking back, she now realized that Sam *did* need a service dog.

While she had been studying to train service dogs, she had seen a couple of men who refused the help of anyone, let alone a dog. It never went well for them. But the one thing she did find useful was taking a step back and letting the veteran come to the conclusion they needed the dog on their own. Vets, especially the men, were always so set in their ways and rigid. Didn't matter that they were disabled in some way or another, they all reacted the same. And it was a reaction.

A reaction to their situation.

A reaction to the emotions they still couldn't control.

A reaction to the realization that they needed help.

Most men didn't think they needed help from anyone. And an injured veteran could act a lot like an injured animal. Sam was going to need time, attention from those he trusted, and patience on her part. Nelly was going to have to let him come to her when he was ready.

This situation was completely different from the one with her brother. For starters, Sam wasn't her brother, or even related to her in the least bit. And she barely knew him. Megan and Jerod would need to be there for him.

Megan walked in and looked around. "What happened?"

The tension in the room was palpable. If Nelly could feel it, then Megan, who was everyone's counselor, would certainly notice.

Skeeter was the first to answer. "Sam's throwing another tantrum. Take a seat so we can start eating."

Nelly blinked a few times. She didn't know Skeeter, but that seemed like an oversimplification of what had just happened, and extremely rude.

"Sam and I had a misunderstanding yesterday, and I think he was surprised to see me here today." Nelly looked to Jerod. "Maybe I should go home."

"No, Nelly. He's got to learn how to deal with his anger better. I'll go talk to him. Y'all start without us." Jerod left the room before the roast was even brought out.

Nelly could feel the door opening behind her, so she moved to the side. Which was a good thing, because Dana was directly behind her with the roast on a giant platter. "Oh, here. Let me help." Nelly put her hands out to steady the tray.

"Thanks. It goes right in the middle of the table." Dana looked relieved once the roast was on the table and nothing had fallen off.

While dinner was tasty, it was also quiet. Well, quiet compared to the last time she had eaten a meal there.

When Jerod returned to the table, Nelly looked up expectantly. "How is he?"

"He'll be fine." With a tight smile, Jerod began to fill his plate.

Nelly regretted accepting the invitation to dinner. She could have easily gone out, or made a sandwich. Just because she didn't have a stove didn't mean she couldn't make any food.

"I think I'm gonna head out to Missoula and pick up a camp stove," Nelly blurted as she was leaving the house. "Any suggestions on where to go for the best deal?"

When Sam had come over the other day, he was supposed to leave a stove and barbeque, but after he learned about why Nelly was there, he left with the stove and grille still in his truck.

"I'm sorry—I completely forgot," Jerod said. "I've got a small stove you can borrow until your house is safe." He left and returned a few minutes later with a large camp stove, the kind that had four burners.

She was grateful for the loan, as he'd also included a tank full of propane.

First thing Monday morning, Nelly was up early and had taken care of the dogs. She'd just finished brewing a pot of coffee when she heard a loud engine chugging up the dirt drive.

When she went to investigate, she couldn't help but chuckle. The black waste management truck was pulling a dumpster larger than anything she'd ever seen. Sam had told her they'd probably fill it up twice, but this one was the size of a mobile home. How in the world could they fill it up twice, let alone once?

Then images of the inside of that death trap of a house haunted her. She shivered when she remembered the bear. The animal control guy was due at eight this morning. Nelly looked at her watched and noticed it was five till eight.

"Hm, good timing. Huh, Spike?"

The dog quirked his head and looked at her as though he was trying to understand her, but just couldn't.

Buffy chuffed and nodded her head as though she did understand.

These dogs gave Nelly so much love and enjoyment. A smile followed her light chuckle. Then she went and picked out four dental bones and gave them each one. That would only distract them for a minute. She needed to get more rawhide bones.

While the dogs were distracted, she picked up her thermal coffee mug and headed out front. She was sure to close the door tight behind her. She didn't need the dogs getting out and taking any issues with the strangers on her property today. Or with the dead bear when they brought it out.

Just the thought of her dogs getting near that biohazard almost made her sick. As she turned the corner of the house, the dumpster was being let down right to the side of the front door, close enough that if they were able to get the front window open they might be able to throw some through the window and out into the bin. Most likely they'd get a chain gang going and that would be how they'd get most of the junk out, but it was fun to think about the men taking turns trying to get the junk inside the bin through the window.

Maybe she could come up with some sort of game and invite the local teenagers to come and help. Free labor would be worth the possible mess. She shook her head when she thought of the liability. It wasn't worth it.

When she stepped to the front porch, she noticed a white truck had come up behind the dumpster and was off to the other side of the house waiting for her.

"Nelly Wilson?" the short, elderly man with a gray combover asked as he got out of his truck.

"Yes, that's me. Are you the man from animal control? Here to take away the bear carcass?" She prayed that was him.

He nodded. "Yes." Then he looked to the dumpster and raised a brow. "You weren't planning to throw the bear out with the trash, were you?"

Her eyebrows shot up to her hairline and she shook her head. "No, sir. I was instructed to leave that room alone until you came and did your inspection. And you'd make sure the body was removed properly. This"—she motioned to the monstrosity of a dumpster—"is for the rest of the house." Her nose scrunched when a scent from the house wafted her way.

"Yes, I hear this house should be condemned." The government employee looked to the door, then back at her. "I'm Francis Anderson."

"Nice to meet you, Francis. Did you want to go and see the body now? I highly suggest putting on a mask first." Nelly wafted a hand in front of her face.

"Actually, I have a suit to don, then I'll be ready." Francis moved to the back door where he pulled out a white suit that looked more like he was heading to the moon than inside her house. Once it was on, he put on a helmet that made Nelly think of Jacques Cousteau as he prepared for deep dives.

The more she thought about it, Francis was heading into something as scary as the ocean's depths. Only this was the depths of a house that might be haunted by the bear who was killed inside it. But that didn't make sense. Ghosts weren't real. And even if they were, bears didn't have souls, so it couldn't haunt her house.

A shiver went down her spine, again. It was shaping up to be a day full of visceral reactions. Once the place was all cleaned up, she'd have to bring in an exorcist. Or maybe just ask the pastor and few deacons to come and pray through the house. Protestants did that, didn't they? Or was it only a Catholic thing? She might have to convert if the local pastor wouldn't pray out the evil that was sure to inhabit her house.

With that sunny thought, she followed Francis when he waved her over.

The suited man took off his helmet and held it against his side. "Here, you might need this to communicate with me." He handed her a walkie-talkie.

"You can hear it in your suit?" She looked doubtful and wondered if he wasn't just making it all into one big joke. How did she know this man was really from animal control? Maybe he was a friend to the guys at the Crooked Arrow Ranch and here to play a joke on her.

"Yes, and I'd prefer it if you stayed out here while I go in and inspect the area." The man put his helmet on and entered the deep, dark expanse that was her house.

Nelly turned her head as she heard the waste management truck leaving. The man never said a word to her, he just dropped off his load and turned tail and ran. She really couldn't blame him.

When the driver got a view of the Jacques Cousteau wannabe he'd probably figured this place was a biohazard, or the house was haunted. She was going with haunted. It was more fun to tell everyone she lived in a deep, scary, haunted house.

Static squawked through the radio and she turned her attention back to the house.

A disembodied voice came over the radio. "Nelly, can you hear me?"

It seemed her mind was really going with the haunting. "Yes, Francis. Are you alright?"

"Yes, ma'am. Did you say the room was upstairs and to the left?"

"Yes, you'll have to climb over quite a bit of rubble." Nelly blew out a breath, grateful she didn't have to go inside—yet.

When a rumble came through the radio and then a smash sounded, she regretted her thoughts. "Francis, are you alright?"

A few moments of silence filled the air and panic started to set in. Nelly took three steps toward the house when a crackling came over the radio. "I'm okay. You weren't kidding about the junk in here."

She heaved a sigh of relief. "Where are you?"

"At the top of the stairs. Heading to the room you mentioned now." Francis gave her a step-by-step account of where he was. And she knew the second he saw the bear.

The man on the other side of the radio gasped, then let out a cry. It wasn't pain, more like sorrow. If Nelly wasn't mistaken, the man was now crying.

Nelly held down the button on the radio. "Are you alright, Francis?"

A couple of sniffles came over the air before he responded. "Yes, it's just so sad. How did the bear get in here to begin with?"

She shook her head. "I don't know. I just bought the house, and when I arrived it was like...well, like a pack of animals had been living in there for years."

"I'm going to have to call this in and get someone to come out and help me. We'll take a few of the bullets from the wall in case we have data on the gun, or guns, that did this. It's illegal to kill a bear and leave it behind like this. All bear shootings must be reported, even if it's done in self-defense."

"I would imagine shooting a bear inside the house would qualify as self-defense." Nelly had no idea how the bear had made it up there, but it had to have been scary for those who were squatting in her house. She was confident she'd had squatters in there before the bear incident. They had probably lived there for years.

When Francis walked out the door, Nelly let out a sigh of relief at seeing him in one piece and not limping.

"I'm going to call the local sheriff and see if he wants the house cordoned off, or just the room." Francis had his white helmet with the metal crossbars over the front plastic windows off and in his hands before the door closed behind him.

Nelly bit her lower lip, hoping she'd still be able to junk the bottom of the house while waiting for Francis, or the sheriff, to do their thing with the bear.

While Francis was on the phone, Nelly heard another vehicle coming up her road. One good thing about living out in the middle of nowhere was that any sound in the area would be noticeable thanks to the natural quiet all around.

The white van from the Crooked Arrow Ranch pulled up next to where Nelly was standing and the doors opened. Jerod stepped out from behind the wheel, Sam from the front passenger seat, and another six men came from the back.

"And here I thought we'd be the first ones to get here. Looks like we're the last." Jerod held out his hand, and Nelly shook it.

"Good morning, Jerod. Thank you so much for all the manpower." Nelly smiled and waved at the men.

Jerod had warned her that some of the men would have various disabilities she might not be used to, and he was right. Thankfully, she was awake enough to recognize that she needed to keep her face natural and smile at all the men.

One of them, Arthur, had an eye patch that had gone askew. She could see he was missing his eye, and the socket was red and swollen. Instead of dwelling on his missing eye, she continued to smile and greet everyone.

Sam, hunched with a frown, grunted his greeting and stood taller before he cleared up the emotions on his face. "I see Francis is here. Can we get inside now? I want to get this started right away."

"Ah, I'm not sure. He just escaped the place and had to call the sheriff." Nelly shrugged and looked over her shoulder at the older man who had just hung up the phone. "Oh, good. He's off the phone. Let's see what he has to say."

It wasn't too bad; they just couldn't go upstairs at all.

"I wouldn't imagine we'd need to go up there for several days anyway," Sam said. "I think it's best to get the entire ground floor cleared before starting upstairs." He headed toward the front door after he took a pack out of the van.

Not really sure what to do, Nelly looked to Jerod. "So, where do we start?"

"I think we need to get our protective gear on and then evaluate the house. But probably should start with the front room so we can clear a path to the rest of the place." Jerod moved to the truck, and his men followed him.

Barking caught Nelly's attention. "I better go see what's got them upset. I'll come join you shortly." She came around the house. "Spike, Ruhig."

The dog stopped his barking on command, but he whimpered for a few more seconds.

Nelly gave him a look that caused him to finally shut up. The dog hung his head and waited for her next command. "Loss das sein." Even though most commands were one word, they all knew the phrase for *don't do that*. And obeyed. She joined him where he sat, inching his way closer to her. When she sat down on the ground, the dog put his head in her lap. He seemed upset, but she couldn't understand why. Unless it was because so many strangers were on the property. That was probably it. Spike was the one dog who was going to need extra training before he was ready to partner with a vet.

Nelly stood up and decided to get the leashes and take two dogs at a time out to meet the men. It would show them that she wasn't in any danger, and neither were they. It might also give her a chance to see the dogs interact with the veterans, and if any of them might bond easily with the dogs.

First she leashed Spike, then she chose Buffy. Rogue and Angel would be last. Spike tended to do better around Buffy. The female dog calmed Spike's inner beast, and she could usually keep him focused on the work when Buffy was with them.

The men had started to go inside the house with their *Ghostbusters*-style costumes on to keep them safe from any dangerous particles in the air. "Jerod, where's the Geiger counter?" She chuckled, and he grinned back at her.

"I think I left it on my honeymoon. I guess I'll have to head back out to get it. It could take me a week or more." The newlywed looked as though he was ready to head back out and take his bride away from all of this.

"Where'd you go for your honeymoon? Three Mile Island?" The idea of anyone taking a Geiger counter on their honeymoon was outrageous. But she supposed there were crazies who still tried to break into Fukushima, Japan, so why not Three Mile Island?

Jerod's smile dropped. "Dana and I want a whole passel of kids, so that'd be a no."

Nelly laughed, and it felt good. After the way the morning had started, it was nice to feel a little bit lighthearted for a change.

Both dogs stood still and were quiet, which surprised Nelly. Jerod must be a dog guy. "Jerod, I'd like to introduce you to Spike and Buffy."

Jerod arched a brow. "Really? Buffy and Spike?"

Nelly rolled her eyes. "Yes, so I was a bit into a *Buffy the Vampire Slayer* marathon when I got the dogs."

"Where's Angel?"

"He's back in the barn with Rogue." Nelly grinned.

"Seriously? Where'd Rogue come from?" Jerod looked down at the dogs and asked, "Can I pet them? Or are they working right now?"

"Thank you for asking first. You can pet them. They're off duty right now. Usually a service dog is on duty when he or she is wearing a vest. When they don't have a vest on it's a sign to both them, and everyone else, that they aren't working." After so many kids and adults trying to pet her dogs while training, she'd started stitching statements on the dogs' vests to alert people that the dogs shouldn't be touched.

While the dogs loved all attention, if a working dog had people loving up on it, it took the attention of the dog away from his or her owner. It wasn't good for the dog to forget that they were on the clock. When service dogs got distracted too much, that was when the patient could get hurt.

And in the case of a service dog designed to help someone suffering from PTSD, if they lost focus the dog might not catch the signs of its human's distress from too much stimuli.

Both dogs enjoyed Jerod's attention. Buffy wagged her tail and licked Jerod's face when he leaned down to pet her. Even Spike gave a little tail wag, and he rarely liked men. At that moment she knew she'd made the right decision to come here, even if her house was haunted, or exposed to some sort of chemical goo.

*Chapter 14*

O f course, Jerod stayed outside playing with the dogs. Sam just about chuffed like he'd heard Rogue do on several occasions. Guilt consumed him when he thought about how he'd reacted to the real reason Nelly and her dogs were here. He knew service dogs were good for many people, it just chafed at him to think they were planning behind his back.

When Sam looked down the hall, he saw through the window that Nelly was coming back out front with Rogue and Angel. Strange how he knew the dogs by sight now. And even stranger was how he wanted to go outside and say hi to Rogue. If he was honest with himself, he liked the dog.

The moment Sam stepped outside on the porch, it hit him that he'd walked out front without any conscious effort on his part. It was just a strong desire to see Rogue that drove him forward. He wasn't sure how he felt about that, but he did want to greet the boxer. He stood on the porch and watched as Nelly introduced both dogs to Jerod.

Once his friend had greeted the dogs, he stepped off the porch and headed to the group.

"Rogue, hey buddy." Sam smiled and pat the dog's head. The dog sniffed his left arm and whined. How in the world did the dog know his arm was messed up? Super smart animal, that one. He leaned down and gave the dog a hug. "I'm good, buddy. No need to worry about it."

"Hi, Sam. I see Rogue still has a strong connection to you, and you to him." Nelly's mouth opened and then closed, as though she was about to say more but didn't.

Sam didn't know what she was going to say, but he was glad she stopped. "Hi, are you ready for today?"

Angel walked to Sam and rubbed his head against the man's right leg.

"Hey, Angel. Are you here to work? Or play?" Sam reached down and rubbed the dog's head right behind his ears.

Angel's tail wagged and his eyes closed. He was in heaven. The reaction of both dogs put a smile on Sam's face and a lightness in his chest.

"Well, I guess we should all go inside and see what's going on and where we should start." Nelly took the leashes for both dogs. "I'll go put these two away and join you inside once I have gloves and a mask."

Once everyone was inside, including Nelly, they all put forth a plan on how to tackle the mess.

"Man, I've never seen anything like this." Mike, the quietest one of them all, shook his head and whistled low.

Skeeter clapped his glove-covered hands and grinned through the clear mask covering his face. "I don't know. I think I saw something like this on *Friday the 13th* a few years back. Remember that movie?"

Nelly laughed and nodded. "I think you might be right. This is definitely the sort of place a scary chainsaw murderer would hide out."

Arthur Landbury, an electrical engineer for the Army, took the lead. "I think we need to first clear the front room and move back from there. But don't get too close to any outlets or sockets. If you find something plugged in, come get me. Or if anything looks like it might be a live wire, get away and holler for me. I don't want to see anyone get hurt here."

"And whatever you do, watch where you step," Dixon added, and stuck his tongue out.

Everyone laughed and started making crude bathroom and outhouse jokes.

"Guys, while Dixon is right, it's not just excrement you need to look out for. If there's any nails or other sharp objects you could end up in the clinic. Best-case scenario you'll get an update to your tetanus, and worst case you'll end up on an IV." Jerod scanned the ground around them, looking to see if he could point out anything dangerous.

"Right there." Sam pointed to an old, rusty spade. "Looks like someone had planned on doing some gardening in here at one time."

"Gross. I don't even want to know what they planned on gardening." Nelly shivered and slid her feet a few feet in front of her, moving a pile of junk as she went. "I've got a box of black trash bags. Maybe we should try and fill those before moving any of the bigger stuff?"

Her phone rang, and she took it from her back pocket. When she frowned at the caller ID, Sam's heart plunged. He hoped it wasn't more bad news.

"Excuse me, I think I should get this outside. Take the bags and I'll come join you shortly." Nelly handed the box of bags to Jerod, who was the closest to her, before she walked outside and off the porch, out of hearing distance.

With one eye on what he was doing and one on the front door, Sam didn't stray too far away. So he was surprised when the local sheriff walked inside. He hadn't even seen the man drive up.

"Sheriff Colton. Good to see you." Jerod walked toward the lawman and put his hand out to shake, but pulled it back and grimaced. "Sorry, it's probably best not to touch anyone right now."

"Probably not." The sheriff had on a face mask and gloves, but he wasn't wearing a hazmat suit like the rest. His eyes narrowed when he looked at the dumpsite all around him. "How'd this place get so bad and none of us noticed?"

If the sheriff didn't know that this place had been taken over by squatters, for years from the looks of it, it meant he and his team weren't doing their jobs. Or, someone on his team had just turned a blind eye to whatever was going on here. Both options didn't engender any trust on Sam's part toward the local law.

Too bad—law enforcement had been Sam's goal when he exited the Army. Well, before he lost his arm.

"Well, it's not like anyone came out here the past few years, is it?" Jerod was ever the peacekeeper. He should have gone into law enforcement.

Although, Sam decided that Jerod was exactly where he should be. There weren't enough places like the Crooked Arrow to help all of the men and women who needed it.

"Well, better point me to the room with the bear." The sheriff shook his head. "Never thought I'd be saying those words together."

Jerod showed the man where to go, and Sam got back to work, looking for Nelly as he did.

He watched her put her phone back in her pocket and head toward the front door. Sam couldn't help but see the look of worry cross her face, or was it frustration? Either way, the moment she walked through the door she replaced her true emotions with a fake smile and covered the lower half of her face with her bandana.

Normally when Nelly smiled the skin around her eyes crinkled, letting everyone know it was a true smile. But now there wasn't even an inkling of a line near her eyes.

"Is everything alright?" Sam asked when Nelly was close enough.

"Sure." She sighed and looked away.

"So, was that the sheriff?" She nodded upstairs. "Should I go up or wait here for him?" Nelly put her gloves back on.

"Probably stay here. Let him do his work and wait for him to come back down here." Sam handed Nelly an empty black bag.

"Do you think I'm going to be in any trouble for that?" She pointed up to the general area where the room was located upstairs.

He shook his head. "No, it's obvious you didn't do any of this. And the sheriff knows you only just arrived. Whatever took place here was before you even put an offer in on this place. If anything, the local lawmen are responsible, not you."

"Really? I would have thought the Realtor who sold me the place would be responsible for this." This time, the skin around Nelly's eyes did crinkle.

Sam chuckled. "You're still miffed at that Realtor, aren't you?"

"You know it. He had to know the shape this place was in. And then the way he treated me when I got to town, well, I hope he gets his comeuppance." Frustration seeped from her body as she reached down for a handful of trash and jammed it into the bag. Then she did it again.

Sam worried the bag wouldn't be able to withstand the pressure she put on the sides as she punched the debris into it.

They worked together in companionable silence, and Sam noticed her movements became less jerky and slower. Her anger was burning away as she worked, which was a good thing. He too found solace in a hard day's work.

Their voices preceded them, and Sam looked up to see Francis and the sheriff discussing the situation as they walked carefully down and around the debris along the stairs.

When they were down on solid ground—well, maybe not solid, but at least it wasn't slippery ground at a forty-five-degree angle—the sheriff asked if they could clear the stairs and a path from the stairs to the front door.

It took almost three hours before the way was clear for the wildlife team who had shown up an hour earlier to get their equipment upstairs and remove the bear. During that time, the sheriff and one of his deputies had been upstairs taking pictures and bagging evidence as though they were investigating a murder.

"It was just a bear, for Pete's sake. Why all the hubbub?" Dixon asked when the bear was finally out of the house and the government types were all clear.

Jerod answered, "Because they take the killing of wildlife seriously here. Especially bears. Had the people who were squatting here just said a bear got inside and they had to shoot it, there wouldn't have been an issue. But because they acted as though they'd committed a crime by staying silent, the sheriff's going to treat it as a crime until they know otherwise."

"I'd hate to see how they react when there's an actual murder." Nelly inhaled then coughed a few times.

The tension in the room had evaporated before the day was over. And Sam was being nice to Nelly; he'd let his anger and frustration go as he worked on the house.

"You know, I didn't think we'd fill up that dumpster once, let alone twice," Nelly said. "But now I'm wondering if we'll need it to be picked up sooner than planned." Once they were outside, she surveyed the large dumpster and looked back at the house.

Sam rubbed his left shoulder. "You know, it might not be a bad idea to get it swapped on Thursday instead, if you can."

A ping sounded from Nelly's back pocket. When she pulled out her phone, she frowned.

"Bad news?" Sam asked.

With a sigh, Nelly put her phone back. "No."

Sam was a little frustrated that Nelly wasn't opening up to him, but they were barely friends. Did he want to really know what was going on with her? Or would it be better to keep his distance?

Either way, Sam knew there was something going on with Nelly.

# Chapter 15

Nelly hurt. There wasn't a single muscle that wasn't screaming for relief. If only she had a bathtub, then she'd be able to soak in a mineral bath. But all she had in the barn was a shower. She was grateful she had a place where she could clean up, but a long, hot bath would have been nice.

Once she was clean and could move a little bit, she went to the dogs and let them out of their kennels. "Okay, it's play time. I'll get your dinner ready while you four go outside and run off your nervous energy."

Nelly knew she treated her dogs more like children than animals, but she also knew that treating them well meant they'd be happy and healthy, and would treat her, or their new partner, well. Just like a human couldn't be at their best when treated poorly, a dog couldn't, either. No animal could give their best if they weren't given the love and attention they needed.

The trick was to find just the right mix of work and play. Then the dogs would do their best and bond nicely with their new partner. The humans she placed her dogs with weren't owners, they really were partners. The relationship between a service dog and the human he or she worked with was more symbiotic than a master/servant relationship. Both parties needed something in order to work well with the other. Which took training.

That was where she came in. Nelly would work with a dog for around eighteen months, sometimes longer, depending on how well the dog took to the work. Then she'd place the certified service dog with a person who needed the partner. Her specialty now was service dogs designed to assist someone with PTSD. While she chose to work with veterans, the dogs could be placed with a civilian who had never served. It wasn't as though a veteran suffering from PTSD needed a dog who was trained differently than someone who had never served but still suffered from PTSD.

Originally, Nelly hadn't chose to work with veterans. But when her brother came back from war suffering from the effects of his time in Afghanistan, she knew what she had to do. It had taken her time, but she'd finally received her first government grant from the Veterans Administration to train service dogs that would be paired with vets.

The VA gave her various options for where to reside and train. But when she heard about the Crooked Arrow Ranch and what Jerod was doing here, she knew this was the place. It was almost as though the Holy Spirit was pulling her to Frenchtown, Montana. As she read the description of the ranch and the area, a feeling of peace finally descended over her. She'd been in such turmoil since her brother died that she wasn't sure where to go next. All she knew was she had to help returning veterans.

Even with the misunderstanding between her and Sam, she was still very grateful she had chosen Frenchtown. Which was why she was so confused over the call and text she'd received earlier that day.

When she left Atlanta, Georgia, she thought she'd severed all ties with Mick Williams. He'd been her boyfriend for almost a year. They had discussed getting married a few times, but when he started talking seriously about marriage, Nelly began to wonder if it was what she wanted.

Well, she did want Mick. But the life he wanted was nothing at all like what she had envisioned. She still remembered the conversation they'd had a few months before she left.

"Honey, you won't need to work once we're married, so why are you stressing so much over those dogs?" Mick's silky-smooth voice always sent shivers down her spine. He was a younger, American version of Idris Elba—tall, gorgeous, and muscular.

The funny thing was that Mick had at one time supported her in her desire to train service dogs. But once they started getting more serious, he began trying harder and harder for her to do it more as a pastime than a true career.

A week before she broke up with him, they were at a charity fundraiser in town. Mick owned two high-end car dealerships in town and was about to start a third. So, he was out at all events where he might find more rich car buyers. But this time, Mick was different. Usually he was proud of what she did, but that night he continually changed the subject back to himself, and her being his "arm candy." He didn't actually use those words, but that was how he treated her.

Not once did he try to help her business move forward. After they finished speaking with a local celebrity who happened to have a cousin that had her own service dog, Nelly confronted him. "Mick, what's going on with you? Abel's cousin is someone I've met before, and her situation is exactly what I train dogs for. Why wouldn't you let us discuss my business?"

"Because, darling, you're not going to be doing that work much longer. Why get anyone's interest in a business you're going to shut down as soon as we're married? They should be looking at other trainers." The condescension dripped from his normally deep, husky voice. The man who had cheered her on for months was suddenly treating her as though her dreams and desires no longer mattered.

Nelly had heard of men who changed once marriage was on the table, but she never though Mick would be that sort of man. And when she broke up with him only a week later, he acted as though it didn't really matter.

He had even said, "There's plenty of women who'll want to be at my side and help me move my business to the next level. If you want to wallow in dog excrement for the rest of your life, so be it."

The very next night, he was out with a supermodel. While Nelly didn't think he'd ever cheated on her, she wondered if he'd ever loved her.

So when he'd called her earlier that day, she was confused. It had been a few months since they'd broken up—why call now? Then, when he texted to confirm their "date" for a call that night, she was worried something might be wrong. The man was trying too hard to talk to an ex-girlfriend.

When eight o'clock rolled around, her phone rang. Nelly had prepared herself a cup of calming peppermint tea. If she was going to have to learn something awful, she'd need the hot drink to soothe her nerves. Shoot, she needed the drink to soothe her overactive nerves now. If she did get bad news, she wasn't sure what she was going to do.

At least she had the dogs to comfort her. They were excellent when it came time to give comfort.

"Hello?" Even though Nelly knew who it was, she was still unsure what was going on when she answered the call, and it came through in her voice.

"Nelly, darling. It's so good to hear your voice. How are you?" Mick's deep, sexy voice sent a thrill down her spine. That was one of the things that had drawn her to him—his voice. Every time they spoke, she pictured Heimdall. He even resembled the actor who played the sexy Norse deity in the movies. Although, Mick was a bit younger.

"Mick, I'm fine. What's up?" She had decided earlier that in order to get through this call, she'd play the cool card. There was no way she wanted him to think his call affected her at all.

"Sweetheart, I've missed you. Have you missed me?" He was always so confident, and he knew she had loved him.

Usually when he called her pet names, her heart warmed up. But this time it felt forced. Or was it always forced, and she had just ignored the warning in her head? "Mick, it's been months. I know you didn't call me out of the blue just because you missed me."

There was a pause over the line, and Nelly wondered if she'd lost the connection. Before she could pull her phone away from her face and check, his smooth-as-silk voice responded, "Baby, I have missed you. I swear." Mick paused, then asked in a lower voice, "have you thought about coming home yet?"

That took her aback. She wasn't prepared for him to ask her to come home. She figured he needed something, but never had she dreamed he'd want her back. "Why?"

"Why what?"

"Why are you all of a sudden asking me if I want to come home? What's going on?" A niggling feeling was budding at the back of her mind. While she didn't know what he was up to, she knew there was an ulterior motive behind this call.

"I told you, I miss you. And I want you to come home."

"And I told you very plainly that I'm not giving up my career. This is what I want to do. And it's important work. But you never understood that, did you?" Frustration began to bubble up, and she was ready to get off the phone with him.

"Sweetheart, I did understand. And I'm sorry I put my career above yours. I don't know why I thought you couldn't work. Most society wives spend so much time on their charities, they might as well be pulling a paycheck. I guess... I don't know. I just must have thought that..." He sighed over the phone, and Nelly could hear him running a hand through his hair.

She loved it when he mussed up his perfect coif. Nelly loved it even more when she was the one who ran her fingers over his longer hair. She had even envisioned him deciding to go bald one day, just like Idris Elba, and she loved the idea of being able to run her hands over his soft, shiny scalp. But that all changed the moment he had decided she couldn't work.

"You just thought you wanted me to be your arm candy, and that in order to do that I couldn't have my own career." The memory still bugged her, and she wasn't about to let it fade. He couldn't sweet-talk her into coming back just so he could get his way.

"I'm sorry. Can you ever forgive me?" For once, Mick did sound repentant. Normally when he said he was sorry it sounded more like a practiced speech. This didn't sound that way.

The nervousness she'd felt earlier had evaporated and been replaced by trepidation. Was he for real? Nelly sucked in a breath. "Are you really apologizing to me?"

"Yes, yes I am. I was wrong to want to change you."

It was exactly what she had wanted to hear in the weeks following their split, before she made the decision to move to Montana. But now that she was here and things were moving forward with her new business, she wasn't sure if it was what she wanted after all. Getting the apology was nice, but did it change anything?

"Thank you. I appreciate that. I really do." What else could she say?

"Baby, does this mean you're going to move home and marry me?" While Mick hadn't actually proposed, they had talked about it enough to know that he was planning on popping the question before she broke things off with him.

"I don't know about that. I have a home here now. And I'm working with local vets to get my current dogs placed, and I have four more dogs coming soon. Everything here is moving forward. My life is in Montana now."

"Darling, I'm more than happy to support you and help you make the move back here. And I do want you to keep doing what you're doing. Couldn't you move home and then just travel when you place a dog with a new owner?" Mick never did quite understand the relationship between a service dog and its partner. Ownership wasn't what that relationship was about.

"Mick, I have a ranch now." Nelly wasn't about to sell this place, even with the nightmare of a house.

"Can you hire some people to work the ranch in Montana for you while you move back to Atlanta to be with me? You can bring dogs here, and have some there. Then you'd have an even larger business than before." Mick was really pushing hard to get her to come home.

While Nelly wasn't ready to leave Montana, she had loved Mick. The question was, did she still love him? And did she trust him to support her and her new venture? "Mick, this is a lot to process. Can you give me some time to think about it?"

"Of course, baby. I love you. But, can you come for a visit? I'd love to see you."

Suspicion began to fill the warmth that had enveloped her, and a chill began in her stomach. "Did you need me home for something in particular?"

"Yes, to be with me. I told you I missed you." He sounded so sincere.

Nelly stood up and began to pace as she tried to get off the phone with Mick. "Let me think about it, alright?"

"Of course, my love."

Now he was putting it on too thick.

Nelly knew there was more to this than just him missing her, but she didn't know what. She'd have to call up one of her old friends and see if they knew what was going on.

*Chapter 16*

When Sam arrived at the ranch Tuesday morning, he could tell something was bugging Nelly. He figured she was still upset with him, and she should be. He had been rude. Although, yesterday all had seemed fine between them. Had she decided to be angry with him again? Women did that. One day all was fine, then the next they'd be mad again for no good reason.

During their group sessions last night, Megan had spoken about dealing with your issues as soon as they arose. Was Nelly his issue to deal with? Or was the tension between them her issue to deal with?

Instead of dealing with whatever this was, Sam decided to get to work. If Nelly wanted to confront him, she could. So he spent the next few hours in relative silence as he and most of the guys from the Crooked Arrow cleaned out the trash, and things he really didn't want to identify, from Nelly's ranch house.

When lunchtime came, Jerod entered with piping-hot pizza boxes. "Chow time!" he called out so everyone could hear him. "Did we lose anyone to the monster of the abyss?"

Everyone chuckled, including Sam. "Or is it the monster from the deep?" Some of the piles had been up to Sam's waist. Most of the junk throughout the house only went up to one's calf, but there were those that went higher. And it was those giant piles that Sam feared held more than just rat excrement. The smell alone ensured he was going to keep his mask and gloves on the entire time he was inside that deep, dark, abysmal hoarder's paradise.

Nelly walked into the front room from the back of the house and scrunched her nose. "You're not planning on eating in here, are you?"

Jerod's face blanched. "Gross. No, I just came in to entice everyone to follow me to the barn."

When Jerod walked out, all of the men and Nelly followed him out single file, heading toward the barn around back.

"I guess he's sorta like the Pied Piper of pizza?" Nelly joked.

Skeeter snickered, and Mike chuckled.

"I'd say that's an apt description of our fearless leader." Sam turned around and grinned at Nelly, who finally smiled back at him. His stomach turned somersaults, and he had a lightness to his step he hadn't felt all day.

Dana had the day off from work, so she had come over and set up folding chairs and a large folding table in the barn. On the table she'd also set up pitchers of ice-cold water and sweet tea. "Help yourself to drinks. Over there"—she pointed to the end of the table—"are the cups, plates, and napkins. But don't forget to wash your hands first." She scrunched her nose and looked at everyone in turn.

"Half can follow me outside, where I have a spigot and soap." Nelly pointed to the little room in the back of the barn. "The other half can go into the kitchen area and wash up."

Sam followed Nelly and was right next to her as they walked outside. As he took his gloves off, he realized that Nelly would be seeing his prosthetic for the first time. Well, other than that little bit of the wrist she'd seen the other day when they had their argument. He wasn't sure how he felt about taking his glove off in front of her. So far, only the doctors at the VA hospitals and the residents of the ranch had seen his fake hand. He hadn't even let his mother see his prosthetic. She asked, but when he noticed the moisture developing in her eyes and the way she sniffed, he knew she wasn't ready to see this part of him.

But Nelly was different. How would she react now that she knew?

They were the first to arrive at the outside washing station. "Here, let me get the water going. It doesn't get very warm out here, but since it's a nice, early summer day, it might be alright." She put her hand under the water and waited until it was comfortable.

Nelly bit her lip and looked from his hand to his face.

Sam knew she wanted to ask a question, but it looked like she was holding back. "Go ahead and ask."

"I'm guessing you don't need help washing up, but is your hand alright to go into the water and get soapy? Do you need any special kind of soap?" Her facial expression was more of curiosity than pity, or fear. And Nelly certainly didn't look like she was about to burst out into tears.

Sam shook his head. "No, I can use most soaps. Just not the antibacterial stuff." He could use that once in a while if nothing else was available, but it was better not to use it.

The smile on Nelly's face lit up her entire countenance. It was as though the sun was shining down on her. Her eyes sparkled, her face glowed, and her white teeth sparkled in the sunshine, almost like a toothpaste commercial. All she needed was that glimmer sparking off a tooth and she would be a walking, talking ad for toothpaste.

It was almost enough to make Sam laugh.

Instead, he shook the thought out of his head and put his hands under the water. It felt nice to have clean water flowing over his hand, even if he could only feel it on his right hand. The warmth of the day filled him, and he let the fear of how she would react flow from his shoulders. An ache he hadn't realized was there until it was gone had left his neck and back.

He focused on the task and worked the soap into his fingers and all over his hands, especially the prosthetic one. Then when he was done, he stepped to the side to dry his hands on a paper towel so Dixon could clean up next.

Sam looked around and noticed that Skeeter had stayed inside to clean up. While Sam liked the cowboy, sometimes the man acted more like a man-child and would ruin a good moment. This was a moment he didn't want spoiled. It was the sort of thing that gave Sam hope. At least, hope that they could be friends without Nelly feeling as though she *had* to be his friend.

It wasn't planned, or at least Sam didn't think it was, but Nelly sat next to him at the lunch table that day and it felt *right*. Her strange mood from earlier in the day had been replaced with laughter and joking.

The rest of the day went almost too well. When they left, Nelly smiled and waved at him. For the first time in a very long time, Sam was looking forward to the next day.

And when the next day came, it went off without a hitch. Well, until Skeeter got lost in a room piled high with something that would have set off a Geiger counter if they had one. Sam was sure of it.

"Help!" a loud and high-pitched voice screamed from one of the rooms in the back of the house.

It was Wednesday afternoon, and the front half of the downstairs was cleared out. As was the kitchen. They were now working in separate areas. Sam had gone upstairs to work on the first bedroom with Nelly. And just when Sam thought he might be getting up the courage to ask her to dinner over the weekend, Skeeter's frightened voice sounded up the stairs.

Nelly's head popped up from the other side of what must have been a bed at one time, but now served as a mini-trash dump. Most of the trash bags had been cut open and the contents strown all over the bed. "Who was that?"

Sam looked out the bedroom door and frowned. "I think it was Skeeter. Wasn't he in the back pantry when we left him?"

Nelly nodded. "Yeah, there were a few large piles, but it didn't seem like anything too bad. At least not compared to this room." Her eyes were watering, and she waved a hand in front of her face.

"Well, if I know Skeeter, he's found a snake, or a rat. Probably alive, too." Sam dropped his bag and headed out the door with Nelly on his heels.

By the time they made their way downstairs, half the team was there laughing. It was a good thing Skeeter was still wearing his entire plastic suit. He lay sprawled out on the remnants of a pile with a dead rat on his stomach and what must have been ten pounds of animal droppings all around him, and on him.

"Oh, Skeeter. How in the world did you end up like this?" Nelly bit the inside of her cheek to keep from laughing. Thankfully, the bandana covered her mouth so he couldn't see the grin she was trying so hard to keep at bay.

"It was like a cartoon in slow motion. I stepped over a pile of rat droppings, only to land on a slimy banana peel. Before I could right myself, I was flying through the air with my legs up higher than my head. I think I might have broken something." The poor man lay there not moving, which said a lot for how bad he must have felt.

Jerod moved the men away from the opening and stepped inside the large walk-in pantry. "Can you move your legs and arms?"

Skeeter moved them all enough to prove nothing was broken.

"Alright, try to get up. But don't do it if it hurts. I want to get you outside and then I'll check you over." Jerod moved closer to Skeeter, in case he had to help. But he'd learned from Skeeter's mistake, and instead of lifting his feet to walk, he slid his boots through the gunk on the floor, releasing a toxic scent that made everyone's eyes water.

"I'm so going to have to strip out all of the flooring and replace the drywall, aren't I?" Nelly asked.

Four different voices replied in unison, "Burn it down."

Sam chuckled, but watched as Nelly flinched and closed her eyes.

"Alright Skeeter, you got this." Jerod put a hand out to help the man up.

Once Skeeter was standing again, they all went outside to watch as Jerod took the hose and cleaned the filthy cowboy off.

If some of that stuff on him wasn't excrement, Sam would eat his hat. "I think his suit needs to be burned after this."

"Maybe not burned—it is made from plastic. But a burial is definitely in order." Nelly had taken her bandana off, and Sam could see her teeth as she grinned at him.

The rest of the week went off without a hitch. A few more dead animals were discovered under the various piles, which helped to account for the atrocious smells in the house, but no one else fell. And no one got sick.

When waste management showed up on Friday to switch out the dumpsters, they were ready for it. The original one had been full to the brim. But thankfully, they had cleared more than half the house.

"Well, I'd say this was a very productive week, wouldn't you?" Nelly asked Sam.

With a nod, Sam finished drying his hands after washing them. "Say, since we all agreed to take the weekend off, how about we..." He couldn't finish what he was about to ask due to the sound of an SUV pulling up out front and the horn honking like the driver's life depended on it.

"Who's that?" With a furrowed brow, Nelly turned toward the sound and left Sam behind.

Sam was disappointed, but also glad he hadn't gotten a chance to finish his question. Not when he walked around the front of the house and saw Nelly in the arms of another man. A man who looked to be from a whole different zip code than Sam would ever see.

Chapter 17

Shock was too mild of a word to describe what Nelly felt upon setting eyes on the one person she'd never in a million years expected to see. "Mick, what?"

He grabbed her in his arms and gave her a bear hug. "Nelly, it's so good to see you." When he pulled back his nose was scrunched, like so many had been all week long. "What's that smell? Were you cleaning the dog kennels?"

A snort-laugh escaped Nelly's lips, but she wasn't the least bit embarrassed. "Something like that." She turned to point out the house and noticed Sam standing at the corner of the house, his arms crossed over his chest and a glare directed right at Mick. For just one second she thought he might be jealous, but immediately wiped that thought from her mind.

There was no way Sam was into her, not with how angry he always was. He probably just didn't like seeing strangers. That sounded more like him.

Mick looked around and his eyes stopped on the empty dumpster. "What's that for?"

"Ah, yes. I guess I haven't explained the condition of the house to you yet." This was one thing she had never thought she'd need to tell Mick. He was the sort that if it wasn't already in pristine condition, he wouldn't get near it with a ten-foot pole. Had Mick helped her find the right ranch house, he would have insisted they come out to inspect the ranch, together. The moment he'd gotten out of the car, he would have gotten right back in and said it would never work.

He wouldn't have been too far off the mark, especially if he'd seen the interior before they started, and before the bear was removed.

"Condition? I'd say this house needs to be demolished if you need a dumpster that large." Mick sniffed the air. "And what is that rancid stench?" His face scrunched as though he had seen, and smelled, the dead bear.

"Ah, that would be the house. It seems the Realtor didn't put up recent photos of the house and never disclosed the actual condition. There were squatters living here for years, if the inside is any indication. And I'd guess some area residents dumped their trash here instead of taking it to the dump." At least, that was what Nelly and everyone else had decided earlier in the week. There was too much stuff in large piles to not have been dumped by various groups of people.

"And you're living in it?" Mick oozed incredulity.

"No, no, and triple no." Nelly waved her hands in front of her. "I'm living in the barn. It's very nice and has an apartment of sorts."

Mick raised his voice. "You're living in a barn!" He pointed his hand to his rental truck. "Get your stuff and I'm taking you home, now."

With hands firmly planted on her hips, Nelly leaned forward and glared at Mick. "I'm not going anywhere. This is my home. I've got a lot of people helping me clean the house up. Until then, the barn is just fine for me and the dogs."

Before Mick had a chance to drag Nelly away, Sam walked up and glared at the newcomer. "Everything alright, Nelly?"

"Sam. Yes, Mick's just upset about the condition of the house, that's all." Nelly narrowed her eyes at Mick, mentally telling him to be good. "Let me introduce you to my..."

"Boyfriend. I'm Nelly's boyfriend, Mick Williams." He stood tall and extended his hand.

Sam looked at it for a second, then shook it. "I'm Sam Marley. Friend to Nelly and her dogs."

If the red blotches on Sam's hand were any indication, Nelly knew they were having the equivalent of a pissing contest. Each was trying to squeeze the other's hand so tight that he would wince first.

She sighed and shook her head. "Alright, enough of that." Nelly pulled the two hands apart and glared at both *boys*. "Mick, we are no longer together. We broke up months ago."

When Mick's nostrils flared, Nelly knew she'd hurt his feelings. A pang of regret coursed through her heart, but he needed to know she wasn't alright with him coming to town and trying to order her around.

"Sam, could you give us a moment?" Mick cleared all emotion from his face and glanced Sam's way.

Sam looked to Nelly, who nodded her agreement.

"Mick, I told you over the phone that I was happy here. And I'm not giving up my business." Nelly crossed her arms over her chest in an effort to ensure her heart wasn't distracted by the handsome and rich man.

Mick put his arms on her shoulders. "Nelly, I understand your need to work. I do. And what you're doing is very admirable. I want to support you if you'll just come home with me."

The soft look in his eyes, the way he touched her, and then that roguish smile of his was doing a number on her heart, despite her will to keep him away from it. Nelly sighed. "Mick, why don't you stay a few days and see what I'm doing here? No matter what, I can't leave until I get this place in order and complete the placement with the dogs. And even then, I don't know if I want to go back. I certainly don't want to go back to the way it was. I'm not arm candy."

"I know, sweetie, and I'm so sorry about how the way things ended. I let the stress of opening another dealership get to me. I promise, I won't do it again." He leaned forward and kissed her forehead.

"How about I show you around, then when I'm cleaned up we can head into town?" Nelly asked. "There's a nice bed and breakfast on the outskirts of town. You should be able to get a room there, unless they're fully booked for the flower show."

Until that moment, she hadn't even thought of available rooms in town for all the visitors.

"I've got a room booked in Missoula. There wasn't anything in this area." Mick looked around and his nose scrunched again. He'd probably gotten another whiff of the house.

While they'd removed a ton of debris, literally, the smell was still overpowering.

"I need to say goodnight and thank the guys for a hard week of work. Then I need a long, hot shower. How about we go into town after that and grab dinner?" Since Mick had come all this way, Nelly couldn't just send him away. And a part of her still missed him. She had tried not to, but she loved him. She had planned to marry him and spend the rest of her life with him.

If his change in demeanor was due to stress, she could forgive that. She'd seen what severe stress could do to people. It was too bad they couldn't have worked through it before she left. Although, if they hadn't broken up, she wouldn't have met all the guys at the Crooked Arrow Ranch...and Sam. A memory of a rare smile he'd given her earlier in the week reared its head, and she felt a momentary pang. She wasn't sure what the pang was for, but she knew she felt something for Sam.

But Mick had flown all this way for her. She owed it to herself, and him, to spend some time with him and figure things out.

"That sounds wonderful. Where should I wait? Preferably somewhere upwind of this stench?" Mick's beautiful smile sent a shiver down her spine.

Nelly began to lead him to the barn after she said her goodbyes and thank yous to the guys for their help. When Sam walked up to her, he was scowling, as usual.

"Mick, can you give me a moment?" Nelly asked.

"Sure, I'll just wait over by the barn." Mick pointed to the closed door.

Nelly smiled and thanked him. Then she turned to Sam. "Sam, thank you so much. I don't know how I'd be able to do all this without you." Nelly put a hand on his right shoulder and gave it a light squeeze.

"So, you're getting back with that guy?" Sam's bold question surprised Nelly.

"Ah, I don't know. But he flew all the way out here, so I'm going to spend some time with him and see how it goes." She shrugged, not knowing what to do.

The cowboy nodded. "Does this mean you're moving back to Atlanta?"

She shook her head. "I don't think so. I mean, my business is here. I know the house..." Nelly looked back at the house and felt her shoulders sag. "It's gonna take a while to get this place in shape. All I can do is plan to get this ranch going."

"Well, have a good weekend. I'll see you first thing Monday morning." He left and didn't look back.

Nelly wasn't sure how to feel about Sam's reaction. And she wasn't sure what she wanted, either. All she knew at that moment was she stank and needed to get cleaned up.

The ride into Frenchtown wasn't long, but it was awkward. Nelly was all cleaned up and smelled nice, but Mick didn't look happy.

"Is everything alright, Mick?"

"Who's that Sam fellow?" Mick kept his eyes on the road, but Nelly could see his face tighten when he said Sam's name.

"He's the foreman, of sorts, for the Crooked Arrow Ranch. He's basically managing the guys working on my house." While she wasn't exactly sure what Mick meant, she had an idea. If he thought she was dating Sam, it could get weird. But since she and Sam hadn't ever been on a date; they were only friends, or acquaintances.

"Are you dating him?"

That took Nelly aback. Could Mick see something between them that she hadn't been able to figure out yet? "Ah, no. I hardly know Sam. I've been here for two weeks and the past week has been spent working hard on the house."

If Nelly was being honest with herself, she had kinda wanted Sam to ask her out. At least until Mick showed up. Now? Her heart and her mind was full of swirling emotions and she had no idea what, or who, she wanted anymore.

"I think he has a thing for you," Mick blurted as they drove down Main Street looking for a parking space. It was Friday night and it appeared there were a lot more people than what she'd expected.

Nelly decided to ignore Mick's statement. Instead, she kept her eyes on the goings on around town.

"Is it always this busy in town?" Mick had to slow as a man wearing a black cowboy hat and clad in all black stumbled out of the bar and grill right into the street. "Are all cowboys drunken fools?"

"I don't think so. But there are a lot of people in town for the flower festival." Nelly didn't know the man stumbling through the street, but she didn't know most of the people who lived in the area. At least, not yet. She had hoped to spend a lot of time here and get to know all of the locals.

"Well, if this is how it's going to be around here, you might as well move home. At least there people stay out of the streets when they're drunk." Mick located a parking spot and maneuvered the SUV into it.

Knowing that wasn't the truth, Nelly ignored his comment. "We won't have to walk far. The good thing about Frenchtown is that it's so small, no matter where you park it's a short walk to anything." A grin spread across her face when she noticed Lottie, the owner of the Frenchtown Roasting Company, out walking with a few other women.

Once Nelly was out of the truck, she made her way to Lottie and the girls. "Lottie, it's good to see you."

"Nelly, good to see you, too. How's the project coming along?" Lottie leaned in for a hug.

Nelly wasn't big on hugs, but when in Rome and all that. "It's coming. We filled one dumpster already, and next week we'll probably fill the next one. But after that, I think the trash will all be gone."

"That's so good to hear." Lottie looked from Nelly to Mick and waggled her brows.

"Oh, sorry. Where's my manners." Nelly pointed to Lottie, and to Mick as she introduced them. Then she introduced Megan to Mick. But the third woman she didn't know.

"And this is Chloe Beck." Lottie motioned to Chloe, who waved and smiled.

"Are y'all out on a ladies night?" Nelly asked.

"Yes, we are. I was going to invite you to join us, but it looks like you have better plans." Lottie winked at Nelly, who felt her cheeks warm.

"Mick is visiting from Atlanta." Nelly looked at Mick, hoping he wouldn't start with the girlfriend or fiancée stuff. Until they discussed it all, he was a friend and nothing more.

"I see Frenchtown is full of beautiful women." Mick winked at Lottie, then turned his attentions to the other women. He gave them all his flirty smile, the one he used to save just for her, or so she thought.

Not that Nelly had anything to worry about, if the tight smile on Lottie's face was any indication. But it did bug her that Mick would flirt right in front of her, especially since he was pressing so hard for her to come home to him.

In that moment, Mick seemed more like smarmy used car salesman instead of the high-end new car dealership owner he was.

"It was nice meeting you, Mick." Lottie turned to Nelly. "Come by tomorrow morning for coffee and we can catch up on all the trash talk."

Nelly knew exactly what Lottie meant—the trash in her house. Rumors were spreading all over town about the stuff they'd found. Some of the bags had the names and addresses of the prior owners of said trash.

One would think the veterans wouldn't have gossiped, but they did. Men seemed to spread rumors just as easily as women did these days, especially in a small town.

"See ya tomorrow. Have fun tonight." Nelly waved to her friends and guided Mick to the local diner. They didn't have much to choose from in Frenchtown. There was the coffee shop, the diner, and a bar and grill. The bar was more grill than bar, except for when they had large events like the flower show. Then the out-of-towners drank a lot. The local Sip 'n' Go also sold food, but it was more like cheap fast food than something you'd sit down and eat.

Once they were seated with their menus and glasses of water placed in front of them, Mick opened his menu and looked at it for a few seconds before asking more questions. "So, those ladies are your friends? Have you had much time to make many friends?"

"Lottie owns the only coffee shop in town. Megan works at the Crooked Arrow Ranch. And you know, that was the first time I've seen Chloe. So no, I haven't really had much chance to meet people." While Nelly had met others, she was right in that she didn't have a lot of time to be social since arriving.

"I see you still have that need for overpriced coffee. I should have known you'd be all buddy-buddy with the local coffee shop proprietor." Mick grinned, then asked, "So, what's good here?"

They spent the next hour eating good food and just catching up. Nelly wasn't the only one who'd been busy lately; Mick had opened his latest car dealership and was already looking at opening another one in Savannah.

"You always did love the coast. Will you move to Savannah once you break ground?" Nelly knew he didn't need to live there, but they had talked on several occasions about moving to the seaside. They'd been out to Tybee Island a few times and they both really enjoyed the island lifestyle. Life was slower on the island, and the air much cleaner than the city.

"I'll probably get a condo there and spend some time in Savannah during construction and for the grand opening, but Atlanta is home."

The waitress interrupted Mick before he could say more. "Have you thought about dessert?"

"No, thank you. I'm full." Nelly patted her belly and sighed contentedly. She couldn't believe how good the food was at the local diner. Especially their taco salad.

"Just the check, please." Mick smiled, but Nelly noticed it wasn't the flirty one he had given Lottie and the girls earlier. Janice the waitress was pretty, but she was rather young. Maybe Mick just wasn't into girls who'd barely graduated high school? And maybe there was nothing to his flirty moves with Lottie earlier.

It was possible Nelly was overreacting. If so, why was she jealous? Unless she did want to get back with Mick?

# Chapter 18

"Sam, let's have a talk." Jerod motioned for the surly veteran to follow him to his office.

"What?" Sam grumbled something else, but it wasn't comprehensible.

Once they were both seated and Jerod's door was closed, the leader of the ranch sat there looking at Sam. He didn't say a thing, just looked at the man long and hard.

Sam squirmed in his seat and felt like a kid who was about to be reprimanded. He had been extra mean that night. It didn't help matters that Megan went out with the girls. He knew that if he had asked her to stay and talk to him, she would have. But Sam also knew that Megan didn't get many opportunities go out with the girls.

The poor counselor spent most of her time corralling him and his lot of angry men. She did get to spend some time with her boyfriend, but at the moment he was busier than a snakeskin dealer at a swap meet, what with the flower festival going on.

"What makes you happy?" Without any preamble, Jerod blurted his question and sat back and waited.

Sam's nose scrunched as though the man across from him had let loose a stinky one after a hot bowl of chili. "Happy? Who's ever happy anymore?"

"I am." Jerod smiled.

Sam grumbled, "Pft, you got yerself a pretty lady who you just married. Of course you're happy right now."

Jerod snorted. "It's not just the love of a good woman that makes me happy."

"Oh yeah?" Sam narrowed his eyes. "Then what? Working with us sorry lot?"

"It's a lot more than that, but yes, working with you does fulfill me." Jerod paused to gather his thoughts. "Have you read much of the Bible?"

This time it was Sam's turn to snort. "Bible? Don't think so. Me and God aren't exactly on speaking terms these days."

"You do know that He wants to talk to you, don't you? God didn't turn his back on you. Mankind has let evil into this world. It's our own fault that we have war and death." Jerod leaned forward.

Sam crossed his arms over his chest and looked away.

"Sam, this morning I read a verse in the Bible and I think it will help you, a lot." Jerod pulled his Bible from the side of his desk and began thumbing through it. When he found what he was looking for, he looked to Sam and caught his attention.

"'A merry heart doeth good like a medicine. But a broken spirit drieth the bones.' That's from Proverbs seventeen, verse twenty-two." Jerod left his Bible open in front of him.

"I don't know anything about merry hearts. At least not anymore. And I doubt I ever will." Sam lifted his left arm. "There's not a good woman on Earth who would want me."

"Sam, that's not true and you know it. There are plenty of women who stuck by their men when they came home missing limbs or eyes, and some even lost more than one. But this verse isn't referring to a wife standing by her man."

"Oh, yeah? Then what is it talking about?" Sam crossed his arms over his chest again and wished not for the first time that he'd never come home at all. It should have been him who died and not his buddy.

"You really don't know, do you?" Jerod shook his head. "God wants to be the one who makes you merry. When you're right with God, that's when he can heal your heart. And when he heals your heart, then you'll have room for someone to love."

"I loved someone once, and I was close to God. But He took it all away when he sent me to Afghanistan and stole my arm." Sam's anger was beginning to boil over. If he didn't get ahold of himself, he'd start spiraling down. And if he did that, he might get kicked out of the ranch.

The only other option would be a group home run by the VA. And he'd never seen one he liked. The moment he had been accepted to the Wounded Warriors home he was in before this place, he promised himself he'd do whatever he had to in order to stay out of the VA's housing. Sam knew they tried, but they were just too overworked at those places. There never seemed to be enough workers to help.

The Wounded Warriors' home was great, until it burned down right before Christmas almost two years ago. When they sent Sam here to the Crooked Arrow Ranch, he wasn't sure what would happen. But after only a few days, he knew he had gotten lucky. This was the best he'd had it since joining the Army. So, Sam closed his eyes and took a few deep breaths. He had to get himself under control, without medication or going off on a bender.

Jerod sat there watching and waiting. After a few minutes he asked, "Are you done feeling sorry for yourself?"

Sam's head jerked up and his eyes opened. "Hey, now." He shook his left arm. "I think I deserve a little bit of understanding, all things considered."

"This isn't about your arm, or your ex. Is it?"

"What do you mean? Of course it is." Sam slouched back in his chair and grumbled how stupid some people could be.

Jerod shook his head. "No, this about Nelly and her old boyfriend being in town, isn't it?"

"What do you know about it?" Sam asked.

"I know you're sweet on Nelly. And if my eyes don't deceive me, she's interested in more than just friendship with you."

Sam snorted. "Yeah, right. Then why is she out with that Mick character right now?"

Jerod chuckled. "Don't you get it?"

With a shake of his head, Sam scowled.

"Mick came here looking for her, but she didn't seem the least bit excited to see him. Did you see the way she greeted him?"

"All I saw was Nelly next to him, offering to take him around town and show him off to everyone." He had been about to ask her out, and instead she was out to dinner with a man who was not only handsome and rich, but had all of his limbs.

"Sam, be real. Nelly's a nice woman. She wasn't about to run him out of town. Of course she was going to be hospitable to the man. He came all this way to see her. You watch, after the weekend is over, he'll be gone." Jerod pointed at him. "And you'll be smiling again."

"What are you talking about? I don't smile." A frown took over Sam's angry face.

Jerod chuckled. "You keep on telling yourself that. But I've seen the way you smile and laugh when she's around." He paused for moment. "Why don't you spend the weekend in prayer and Bible study? It's time you got back to your Christian roots. Ask God to forgive you..."

Sam interrupted, "I don't have anything to ask forgiveness for. He's the one who needs to ask for my forgiveness. He sent me into war and let a bomb explode by my truck. Why was it I was injured in that explosion, but it was Henry who died a few months later?" He moved to the edge of his seat and raised his voice. "Explain to me how I'm still alive, but a great man like Henry died in my place?"

A lone tear made its way down Jerod's face. "This is the heart of the matter, isn't it? You've been carrying around survivor's guilt this whole time. You think God spared your life only to take Henry's?"

Sam jerked back in his chair and wiped the tears from his cheeks. He didn't need to say anything; Jerod had nailed it on the head.

"That bomb, and the insurgents, they've broken your spirit. And taken not only your arm, but your good friend. Don't let them keep taking from you. The longer you keep ahold of your anger, the more they win. You're a fighter, Sam. I know you are. You wouldn't have survived the bomb to begin with if you weren't a fighter." Jerod pounded his fist on the table and narrowed his eyes. "Fight for yourself now. Fight to get your relationship right with God. Don't let the enemy stay between you and your Lord. You know this deep down inside."

Sam jerked his head from side to side. "No."

"Yes. God loves you. He wants to heal your broken spirit. Let Him, and He will. Think back to your Sunday school classes. Remember the song, 'Jesus Loves Me?' Jesus loves you and He wants your heart to be merry and your soul full of joy. Fight your way back. Because if you don't, then you're giving the win to the devil." Jerod sat back and relaxed his shoulders.

Sam felt something coming from Jerod, but wasn't sure what it was. The man had exuded strength just now, and something else. Was it the Holy Spirit working through Jerod to get him back on the straight and narrow? He wasn't sure, but one thing he was sure about: Jerod was right. He needed to fight for himself.

"You—you'd make a great motivational speaker. Have you ever considered traveling around from VA hospital to VA hospital speaking to the returning veterans? Or maybe even going to the group homes?" One corner of Sam's mouth quirked up in a half smile.

Jerod's body was drained, and he slumped in his chair.

For a moment, Sam worried that the man might be ill and he stood up. "Are you alright?"

"I'm alright, just tired." Jerod ran a hand down his face. "This type of thing takes a lot out of me. I'd never be able to give speeches like that on a regular basis."

"I'm sorry. And thanks." Sam put his hand out, and Jerod shook it. "I'm gonna go to my bunk and maybe do some reading. You're right, I am a fighter and I need a battle plan."

"I'll pray for you, man. God bless."

Sam looked back over his shoulder. "Thanks, Jerod. I think I could use all the prayers I can get right about now."

Before heading to his room, Sam found Dana and sent her to see if Jerod really was alright. Sam knew he was a handful; Megan had told him enough times. But at that moment, he worried that he'd caused too much trouble for Jerod. No matter how mad he was at the world, at God, or even himself, he never wanted for Jerod to be hurt or sick. The man did too much good. He had to stay strong and healthy.

Jerod also had a new wife to take care of. And eventually, they would have kids. Or at least, Sam hoped they would. He'd heard Jerod and Dana discussing future kids. Both wanted a lot of them. Maybe that was what he'd pray for, that God would keep them both healthy and give them a large family. Jerod was going to make a fantastic father, Sam just knew it.

For the rest of the night and all through the weekend, Sam did his chores but kept close to his bunk. He did some praying, but he also opened up the Bible that each person at the ranch was given last Christmas. He hadn't been too happy to get a Bible as a gift. But now he realized that God was preparing him for this weekend.

"God, I don't know what you want from me, or why you had things go down the way they did in the sandpit, but I need your help. I want to fight, I really do. But I'm so tired of fighting all the time. Can you take over?"

A memory entered Sam's mind. Growing up, his parents had this picture on the wall in their hallway. It was of a sandy beach. At the beginning of the print there were two sets of footprints, and halfway down the beach there was only one. Printed on the upper portion was something about God carrying us through the most difficult times. Sam needed to be carried.

"God, will you carry me through this?"

A small bit of the proverbial bricks he was carrying by himself left his shoulders, and he felt as though God was trying to get through the wall Sam had built around his heart.

Maybe, just maybe, God would carry him through the rest of this fight.

*Chapter 19*

It was a beautiful Saturday afternoon and Nelly was working with her dogs. They were doing quite well and she knew that soon she'd need to start bringing in the veterans who needed help. On Monday she had a meeting scheduled with Jerod to discuss which of his veterans would be best suited for a service dog.

The one candidate she hoped would be on that list was Sam. Rogue had already taken to the curmudgeon, and if she wasn't mistaken, she believed Sam returned the affection for Rogue.

Spike was going to need more training, and a woman. Nelly knew he'd never partner well with a man. And it was of the utmost importance for the dog to bond with his human if he was going to be of any help. If she was back home in Atlanta, she'd probably find a child who needed a service dog. Spike had seemed to do well around kids, no matter the sex. Maybe if he was paired with a little boy he'd lose his aversion to men in time.

But they weren't back in Atlanta, and she wasn't sure she wanted to go back to Atlanta. Last night had been nice. Seeing Mick brought back so many memories, and emotions. And not all of them were good. But she'd promised to spend time with him this weekend, and that was exactly what she would do. In fact, she needed to get cleaned up if she was going to be ready in time.

Mick was coming to get her and take her to the flower festival. The thought of Mick smelling the various types of flowers on display put a smile on her lips. This was looking to be a fun weekend, which was exactly what she needed before heading back into the cesspool of the house she had to clean up.

Mental images of the various items they'd found this past week sent chills up and down her spine. And they weren't the good kind of chills, either. It felt more like watching a horror movie.

"No, get your head in the game, girl. Stop thinking about what was and look to what might be." Nelly had to give herself a pep talk to get out of her crazy thoughts. Spike was next to her, nudging her thigh.

"You're such a good boy, aren't you?" The dog always seemed to know when she needed a little push, or some loving. Nelly leaned down and hugged the service dog before putting half of them back in the barn. She had decided today would be a great day to bring Rogue and Spike. They needed more time with strangers and crowds. The flower festival was a perfect venue for training dogs.

If they weren't service dogs, and if her ranch grounds were safe, she would have let Angel and Buffy roam free. But she hadn't had time yet to survey the entire property. Who knew what she might find out back. While the paddock fence kept the dogs in when she was around, she knew they were curious creatures at heart. And the moment she left them loose in the paddock, they'd find a way to either jump the fence that was only ever intended to keep horses inside, or find a loose board to push out.

So, when she left the ranch, they had to be put inside the barn. At least she didn't have to lock them up in the kennels. She only had to lock up the barn and close her make-shift bedroom. Buffy and Angel could have free range of the rest of the barn without any issues.

An hour later, she was sitting in the passenger seat of the fancy SUV driving down her dirt road. Rogue and Spike were being good and laying down in the backseat, that she had covered with a blanket. Mick always did have great taste in cars, but she was starting to wonder if his tastes and hers didn't mesh too well anymore. Nelly was happy with her used truck. Granted, she bought a truck that was only a couple of years old and had low mileage on it, but still, she didn't need anything flashy.

Mick, however, only drove flashy cars and SUV's.

"So, tell me, what should I expect from this flower show?" The side of Mick's face had a few lines creased from the smile she knew he wore. One of the great things about Mick was the fact that he smiled so much. The man almost always had a smile pasted on his face.

Nelly had never wondered if it was real or fake until now. An almost sarcastic tone was coming from him and she wasn't sure what to think.

"Well, there will be a variety of flowers that bloom this time of year in Montana." Nelly chuckled. "Lots of fair food. I heard they have at least four food trucks who practically begged to be a part of this festival. It seems they had quite the turnout for the Christmas trees this past year and now all of their planned festivals have a great list of the region's best food trucks."

Nelly looked at Mick, to see if she could pick up any expressions from him that might tell her what he was really thinking. The man kept his eyes ahead on the road, which was a good thing. In this part of the country one could never tell when an errant cow, or bull, was going to pass by. She had heard one of the local ranchers raised sheep, and a few of them always seemed to get out right before sheering season.

"Maybe they should get one of those reality shows to come out here and film the food trucks. I hear some of those trucks are run by gourmet chefs." Crinkles formed around the side of Mick's eye and Nelly knew his smile was real. His voice lost the almost sarcastic tone, and he seemed truly interested now.

"Not a bad idea. Maybe I'll suggest it to Cody when we see him." Thoughts of camera trucks and throngs of people coming to the ranch flittered through her mind as they road on in companionable silence. Nelly knew that just last year, the Big Sky Christmas Tree Farm almost went under. But with a few new ideas, and help from the local news station, they had come through the end of the year in the black, finally. And this year they were trying out all sorts of different events. The type of thing that would bring local families, as well as tourists looking for something fun and unique to experience in the wilds of Montana, besides a rodeo.

When they pulled up to the Big Sky Farm, recently renamed for the months outside of Christmas, Nelly's eyes flew open wide. "Whoa. There's a lot more people here than I expected."

Mick rode his breaks as he looked for the parking attendants. "I think I expected something smaller, more simple. Do you think they have valet?" His head swiveled from side to side as he scanned for signs telling him where to go.

"Uh, no. I don't think they have valet in this part of the world." She couldn't help it, Nelly had to chuckle at the thought of some teenaged rancher parking the giant SUV that seated seven and still had plenty of room in the back for shopping, or sports equipment. This SUV was the twenty-first century version of a Beverly Hills soccer mom's van. All they needed was four kids who each had their own sport, and they'd fit right in at Rodeo Drive.

"Look," she pointed to a small green flag waving. "I think that's where we are supposed to park." There wasn't even a person holding the flag, it was waving in the wind atop a *park here* sign.

"A bit provincial, don't you think? Where do we go to pay for parking?" Mick turned at the flag and found a larger spot to park, down towards the end of the row.

"Ah, Mick, I don't think they charge for parking in this part of the world." That was one thing Nelly didn't miss about living in a big city, paying for parking. Or paying to use tollroads. She hadn't seen any of that since arriving in Western Montana. It might be a thing in the larger cities, but she hadn't been to any of them, yet.

"They're missing out on a lot of cash by not charging to park. Or better yet, offering a valet service." Of course, Mick always chose valet. In fact, Nelly remembered that he almost never went anywhere unless they had valet.

So why was she so in love with a man who put so much stock into money and prestige?

Mick came over and opened her door for her. He took her hand and helped her down out of the massive vehicle. Then he gave her a rueful smile, brought her hand up to his lips, and kissed it. His lips were warm and familiar against her skin. And she felt the beginnings of fluttering in her stomach. Her old friends, the butterflies, had made a reappearance. This was one of the things she had loved most about Mick – he was the epitome of a gentleman. The handsome man always opened doors for her, he always helped her out of the car, and never let her pay for anything when they were together.

It wasn't that she needed him to open doors or pay for things, but it was those little things that she had never experienced before. No, that wasn't completely true. Nelly had dated men who would on occasion open doors, or pay for meals. But they were never consistent. While Nelly would be happy to pay for meals or go Dutch on occasions, she did still believe in the magic of a gentleman opening a door, or letting the woman walk through first. Those little things that men did all through time to let the woman know she was valued, and precious to him. That's what always set her stomach fluttering.

And it was going again.

Nelly opened the back door and after putting the "In Service" vests on her dogs, she took them out and clipped the leashes on. She knew that her dogs would be welcomed even if she didn't have the service vests on, but she wanted to ensure that the patrons of the festival didn't interfere with the dogs working. And it was also a sign to the dogs themselves that they were on the clock.

Without a word to the dogs, they moved to one side of her and waited for her to walk. They were trained to walk by her side and she put them on her left for today. Mick was on her right.

Once they were headed in the right direction, Mick put his arm around her waist and pulled her close. It wasn't a caveman move. You know, the kind where a guy only pulled the woman close when he thought another man was eyeing her too closely. No, Mick did it when no one was looking, or when everyone was looking. He just liked to be close to her.

And she ate it up.

When a man showed in little ways how much he valued her, she felt loved and wanted. Didn't all women want to feel like a princess with the man they were with?

Mick knew exactly how to do that.

Nelly smiled up at him and leaned her head into his side just enough to show her appreciation. His hand tightened for just a moment on her waist, letting her know he noticed, and liked it.

They had been together long enough to know each other's love languages. Touch was something they both appreciated. It was nice to share a love language with the one you were with.

So where did it all go wrong?

And was he really here to win her back? Or was there something else behind his motivations to bring her back to Atlanta?

Only time would tell.

# Chapter 20

The crowds were louder than Sam expected. He didn't usually have much of an issue with loud noises, or lots of people. Not like some of the residents of the Crooked Arrow did. But, he understood what his fellow veterans were going through. Looking around at the chaos that was the First Annual Big Sky Farm Flower Festival, he felt his chest tightening and his mouth drying.

Sam hadn't felt so nervous in a crowd for well over a year. Probably closer to two years. He had to get out of there, find somewhere safe and quiet. Then he could do his breathing exercises and go through the old mental safety drills. He used to imagine himself back home, with his old girlfriend. Sadly, that wouldn't work these days. He was going to have to find a new happy place. Somewhere that meant peace and safety to him.

The Crooked Arrow Ranch flashed through his mind, and his pulse began to slow. He thought about the horses they rode, the cows they milked, and the friends he was making. Well, they may not call him a friend, but Sam would think of them as friends.

Just as he was around a corner and away from the screaming kids, another image flashed through his mind. This time, it was of a woman with brown hair and deep brown eyes that made him think of hot cocoa on a cold night. The idea of snuggling up in front of a fire as they sipped hot cocoa with marshmallows on top flitted through his head.

Sam stopped that image right away. He shook his head. It wasn't a memory, but a fantasy. He had no business thinking about Nelly that way. She was too good for him. And if that Mick fellow got his way, she'd be in Atlanta next week. He'd probably never see her again. But that might be for the better. For her at least.

He'd love to get to know her better. Again, he shook his head. No, he couldn't do that. The more he got to know her, the more he wanted to kiss her. And that would lead nowhere, fast. Well, it would lead her nowhere, but him to a broken heart. He swore he'd never fall for a woman again after the *she-demon* broke his heart.

He re-focused, back on the ranch that had become his home. He'd have to leave soon, but until that time came, he was calling the Crooked Arrow *home.* It was the only place he's felt safe since returning from war. Which was probably why he hadn't left yet. He was as healed as he was going to get, so he should leave.

It's not like a man can grow back a limb. He just has to learn to live with the replacement and figure out how to work. Sure, he had his disability from the VA, but that wasn't enough to live on these days. Even in Montana rents were high. And forget about buying something nearby. Thanks to those

California rich software geeks who have moved in and taken over most of the state, real estate was no longer affordable for the average guy.

Which was why he wanted to learn everything he could about ranching. If he could get himself working well, he knew he could find a job somewhere on a ranch. Even if it was only part-time or seasonal, it would help to supplement his income. And it would keep him so busy that he wouldn't have time to wallow in his sorrows, which he had plenty of.

It would also keep him from seeing Nelly with Mick. Sam's heart stopped when he saw the smile on Nelly's face as she looked at Mick. She was radiant, like a woman in love. He never had a chance with her. With his back to the wall of the barn, he turned his head and looked out to the pasture behind the barn. The Big Sky farm kept a few horses and some cows. Looking at them would keep him from thinking of her. Or so he thought.

Images of Nelly's smile and laugh when they'd been together rolled through his mind and he felt his shoulders sag. How in the world was he going to stop thinking of her?

Just then a hand gripped his shoulder. "Hey, man. I've been calling you."

Sam jumped and turned around, eyes wide and fearful of an ambush. His right arm went to his chest and he breathed in and out heavily until he could get his breathing under control.

"Sorry, man. I didn't realize I'd scared you. I should have known." Skeeter winced and took a few steps back. "Are you alright?"

Sam could only nod as he worked to get his breathing under control.

"It's the crowds, huh? They getting to you, too? That's why I'm back here. I wasn't expecting so many people to come and see flowers." The younger cowboy ran a hand down his face and looked back over his shoulder.

Sam noticed the young man shiver and then turn to look out at the canvas set before them. Brown and black horses shook their manes while they too seemed not happy about the crowds. The cows, however, continued eating the grass and ignoring everyone else. One was even laying down and sleeping from the looks of it. "Wouldn't it be nice to be so oblivious to all these people?" He looked pointedly at the sleeping bovine.

With a nod, Skeeter agreed. "You know, it was even crazier at Christmas, but then I expected it to be wild. So, the crowds were fun during Christmas. Now," he sighed, "I don't know if I should stay or go back to our ranch."

"I hear ya. I think it boils down to expectations and preparations. But, we told Cody and Daniel that we'd be here to help out. Maybe we just need some time to adjust our thinking? Do you think that will help?" Sam looked to Skeeter, hope filling his eyes that the younger man would have a solution.

"Maybe we should call Megan? What do you think?" Skeeter asked.

"I don't want to bother her. She's here having fun with her fiancé." Sam leaned against the fence separating him from the animals. While he knew that he could call Megan anytime he needed, he also knew she worked hard. Today was supposed to be a day she had off to enjoy the festival.

"I think Daniel's working. It looks too busy for him to take any time off today." Skeeter scratched his head and looked around as though he was searching for something, or someone.

"You looking for Megan?" Sam asked.

"Yup."

Sam sighed then looked at his watch. "It's lunchtime, she's probably over by the food trucks."

"Mmm, that sounds good. Wanna join me for lunch? Food usually puts you in a better mood." With a lazy grin, Skeeter shoved Sam's shoulder lightly.

"Hey, now, I resemble that remark."

"Okay, bear-man." Skeeter led them both to the area with the food trucks, trying to joke around as they walked through the crowds they weren't expecting.

Megan noticed them first and waved them over to her table. "You two looking for food?"

"Aren't we always?" Sam joked.

She arched a brow. "Well, someone seems to be in a good mood."

"Not really. The bear here," Skeeter pointed at Sam, "is in need of food to calm his savage beast."

"Ah, yes. Why don't you two go grab something and I'll save you both seats here with me." The counselor patted the bench next to her and then watched as they walked away.

"You think she knows something's up?" Sam asked once they were in line for stuffed potatoes.

"I do." Skeeter nodded.

With plates full of giant, Idaho potatoes stuffed to the gills with bacon, sausage, cheese, butter, sour cream, and topped with steamed broccoli, the two men grinned when they sat down.

"So, do you think we can eat this whole plate?" Sam asked Megan.

Her eyes widened as she took in the meal fit for warriors. "I think that if you finish that off, you're going to waddle home."

"Nah, this is just the appetizer. After this, I think I'm heading over for a buffalo burger. And then after that, maybe I'll grab one of those slices of pie on a stick." Sam stuffed a fork full of potato into his mouth and moaned. "Thith ish goooood." He added with a mouth full of food.

Skeeter snorted and dug in. "I think I'm going to add one of those funnel cakes with strawberries and cream."

Sam swallowed his food and nodded. "I think I might have to do that, too."

Megan groaned and shook her head. "Didn't your mommas teach you any manners?"

With a piece of bacon hanging out the side of his mouth, Sam shrugged. Then he pushed the piece of pork heaven in his mouth. "What? This is how the drills taught us to eat in basic. If we didn't shove it all in and talk around full mouths, we didn't have time to finish our food."

Skeeter nodded, then added, with a mouth full of stuffed potato, "We all do this."

"Not at the ranch you don't." Megan frowned and added, "I don't want to see this display of poor manners again. You two need to set an example for the rest. They look up to you."

Sam looked to Skeeter, then back at Megan. "Really? They look up to Skeeter? What for, advice on how *not* to woo a woman?" He elbowed his friend good naturedly.

"Hey, now. You're one to talk. I don't see you wooing any women." Skeeter could give it just as good as he took it.

"I don't know. I think he might be ready to woo someone." A slow smile spread across Megan's face and she winked at Sam.

Sam frowned and then grumbled something unintelligible under his breath.

"Oh, that pretty dog trainer?" Skeeter asked. "I can see it." He nodded.

"She's back with her ex." Without realizing it, Sam's flat voice conveyed his displeasure to the group.

Skeeter put his fork down and stared at Sam.

Megan's eyebrows rose so high, they were no longer visible under her bangs. "Really? Since when?"

Sam pointed to a couple across the food area. "Since now."

The other two turned their heads just in time to see Nelly laughing with a handsome man they'd never seen before.

"Who is he?" Megan asked.

"Mick something or other. He's from Atlanta and wants her to go home with him." A sickening feeling filled his stomach and Sam pushed his plate away, only half eaten. "I'm full. I think I'll head back home."

Megan put her hand on his arm. "Wait. Why don't we take a walk and talk about this?"

"What for? It's not like we were dating or anything." Sam pulled away and made to stand up.

"Sam, we need to discuss this." Megan's tone brooked no argument.

Skeeter stood and took his plate. "I think I'll go finish this elsewhere." Then he looked down at Sam's plate. "You done with that?"

Sam nodded. "Go ahead."

Skeeter walked away grinning as he took both his plate, and Sam's to another table and worked hard to finish both meals.

"At lease someone has a hearty appetite today." Sam mumbled.

"Sam, let's go get a cold drink and take a walk. We can head toward the horses where it's quieter." Megan led them away.

Once they were over by the horses, oddly enough, in the same place Sam was when Skeeter found him earlier, Megan cleared her throat. "Care to tell me what you're thinking?"

"Not really."

"Come on, Sam. You know the drill."

With a sigh large enough to spook the horse closest to him, Sam began, "I'm not good enough, anyways. So what does it matter?"

"Sam, you are more than good enough for the right woman. Shoot, any woman would be lucky to have you. When are you going to realize that just because you have a prosthetic arm doesn't mean you aren't man enough for anyone?"

Sam turned quickly toward Megan, practically spitting fire like a dragon. "Because, that's exactly what my ex told me when she broke up with me."

Megan was taken aback and gaped at Sam. Then she composed her shocked expression. "If your ex-girlfriend broke up with you because you lost an arm in the war, then she's not woman enough for you. You can do so much better if you only believe in yourself."

"Then why aren't women falling over themselves to get my attention like they do with Skeeter?" Sam crossed his arms over his chest. Not an easy thing to do for a man with a plastic arm. Instead of folding his right-hand fingers under his left bicep, and rolling his left hand on top of his right bicep, like any other right handed man would, he had to do the opposite. But it was too difficult to get his wrist to move in a way that didn't cause his fingers to jab into his side, so he put his gloved left hand on top of his right bicep. It wasn't nearly as comfortable as it used to be. So he rarely left his arms crossed for long.

With a slight tilt of her head, Megan studied Sam. "Do you really not know?"

He shook his head.

"It's his attitude. Skeeter is overly outgoing. His antics attract the attentions of young women. And he's a flirt. He'll flirt with any woman who looks at him, no matter how pretty, or young. In fact," Megan's lips tilted up, "Just last week I caught him flirting with old Mrs. Morris at the general store. That woman must be old enough to be his grandma."

The grim expression Sam was holding began to break and his eyes lightened just a bit. "She is too old for him. Or maybe I should say he's too young for her?"

"Both." Megan chuckled. "But you can't compare yourself to Skeeter. He's one of the biggest flirts I've ever met, and totally an extrovert. You my friend, are an introvert. It's different for men like you."

"You mean it's different for men who aren't whole."

Megan interrupted him. "No, that's not what I said. We've talked about this before. You're an introvert. It's your personality type. You don't make friends and talk to people as easily as someone who's an extrovert. It's nature. And it has nothing to do with whether or not you have a human arm or a man-made one."

Again, Sam grumbled, and he hung his arms at his side. "I don't know."

"Yes, you do. Think about before you joined the Army. Did you find it easy to talk to strangers?"

With a shake of his head, the tension began to leave Sam's body and his shoulders relaxed. Then he looked out at the horses and put his arms on the top of the fence and leaned in. "I guess that might be true. But women always look at me with pity once they see my left arm."

"Not all women do, Sam. And the women of our generation aren't accustomed to seeing prosthetics. Not yet at least. For some it is a shock. But not all women will pity you. You have a lot to offer a woman. Don't sell yourself short. When you meet the right one, she won't have any issues with your arm. And you won't see pity in her eyes."

# Chapter 21

As they walked around the festival, adults and children smiled and waved at her dogs. Both Rogue and Spike looked around, but not for attention. They were on duty and they were looking for anything that might be in Nelly's way, or might cause harm. Their ears were alert and their snouts up in the air sniffing all of the wonderful scents.

Nelly knew they needed to eat lunch, so just before noon, she took them to an area that had a picnic table off to the side. There, she tied the leashes to the table and took her pack off. She had packed them small travel bowls and food along with bottles of water.

"Should I go and get us some lunch?" Mick asked as he watched her set up the meal for the dogs.

"That would be great, whatever you're having is fine with me." Nelly gave him a quick smile over her should and then got back to work. She didn't normally feed the dogs lunch, but she knew they would be around a lot of food today and so she packed them a special treat. One she hoped would keep them satisfied so they didn't go looking for scraps on the ground. Or children to beg food from.

After lunch of bison burgers and soda, Nelly took Mick to the funnel cake truck. "Care to share one of these with me? I can never finish one on my own."

Mick looked at the truck. "Funnel cake? Isn't that for kids?"

With a small shake of her head, Nelly disagreed. "I think that we can all eat funnel cakes once in a while. I know, it's not cheesecake. If you want one, they do have cheesecake on a stick. But be warned, it's deep-fried."

Mick rolled his eyes. "Are all of the desserts deep-fried?"

"Pretty much. This is fair food after all." Nelly walked up to the window and placed an order for a large funnel cake with strawberries and whipped cream.

Once it was ready, they sat on a bench and ate quietly. However, the dogs wanted a taste. Spike chuffed and Rogue barked once. They both were on all fours staring at Nelly with their tongues lolling. She never gave them human treats, but they did always seem to smell the sweet sugary scents.

"Sitz." She commanded the dogs, who obeyed. "Ruhig." She commanded they be quiet and they were, for the most part. Spike did let out a couple of whimpers, but when she glared at him, Spike was quiet.

After a few moments of the dogs sitting patiently, she pulled out the jerky treats she had been saving for them. She gave each dog two treats and they were happy, if their tails wagging in the dirt was any indication.

After she put their treats away and went back to eating her own treat, Nelly looked around and appreciated all of the families there on the ranch. She was glad that the tree farm looked to be having a good year and wouldn't have to sell.

When Nelly first heard about the local Christmas tree farm, she imagined herself heading there the first week of December and choosing her own tree for the first time to cut down. She'd always purchased pre-cut trees or had fake trees. Living in the city didn't really give her much of a chance to cut her own tree.

She'd also heard about their craft fair and looked forward to buying homemade gifts for friends and family. Maybe even learning how to crochet a scarf. But if she left for Atlanta, that wouldn't happen. However, if she stayed here, she and Mick wouldn't be able to be together. And Mick would never agree to move to Montana. Even if he didn't have his car dealerships back in Georgia.

But she loved Mick.

They continued to eat in silence and Nelly noticed Mick was doing his best to eat half of the deep-fried dough. She stayed quiet until the last bite. "So, I take it you like funnel cake?"

Mick chuckled and that deep sound of his did funny things to her stomach.

"I guess you're right. Even adults can enjoy a good funnel cake once in a while." Mick handed Nelly the last bite. "Here, you should have this."

Just one more thing Nelly loved about this man. He was always so generous. Most men would eat the last bite without even thinking about it. But not Mick. He always did that when they shared dessert.

"Let's go and check out the flowers." It was the reason for the festival, after all. So far, she and Mick had seen all the food offerings and a few craft booths. The festival didn't have a lot of booths, but what they did have was nice. She'd have to see if the patriotic wreaths were still for sale after she got the house fixed up. Right now, there wasn't any room for decorations in the barn. And until she had the house in a livable condition, she wasn't about to put anything inside it. It would be her bad luck to put something pretty in that mess and it end up with lice, or mold, or who knew what disease was in that place.

But, Mick had picked up a hand-tooled leather wallet. She was glad that he'd bought something. If she was still here when they did their next event, she'd buy something. Today, however, was all about the flowers. "Do you think they sell dried flower bouquets?" That was something she could put in the little kitchenette.

Mick looked around and said, "I don't know. After we walk through the flowers, let's see. That might help to spruce up your barn." He grinned at her.

Nelly leaned in against his arm and laughed. "You know, I thought the same thing."

The gardens were long and narrow. Cody and Daniel had taken a small section that had been sitting sallow for the past year, where Christmas trees should have been planted a couple of months back. Instead, they planted a variety of flowers that would bloom just in time for a June flower show.

Nelly and Mick were walking through with the rows of snapdragons and talking about nothing in particular. She had been so happy when he showed up. But they didn't seem to be on the same page anymore. Was it because of Montana? Had she finally found where she belonged? Or was it that they just needed more time to find their new equilibrium together? She still had feelings for the handsome man, but there was something she couldn't put her hand on that felt...off.

The sun was already starting to set, creating a watercolor in the sky of blues, whites, and oranges in the sky. Nelly felt as though this was the place to be. Even her dogs enjoyed coming out to the flower farm. Of course, they had so many scents to snuffle up, they couldn't *not* love it. Bringing them out here to learn to work among strangers had been a great idea.

Currently, she had Rogue and Spike with her, even though neither seemed very interested in Mick these days. At one time, they had liked her old boyfriend. Maybe their instincts reminded them that he'd hurt her, once. Not physically, but emotionally when they broke up. Turning her thoughts to better memories, she walked closer to a row of pink and coral flowers. Both dogs sniffed and turned their heads as though the scent of flowers weren't appetizing.

"I love this flower farm. I can't believe how much Daniel and Cody have done with the Christmas tree farm in only a few months." Nelly leaned down and brought a coral-colored flower up to her nose. It smelled like summer. She'd heard someone once describe the flowers as having a bubble-gum scent, but to her it was fruity and light. A bouquet of these flowers wouldn't overpower a small room, like say a lilac might.

"I'll plant you an entire garden once we're married." Mick took her hand and brought it up to his lips. He barely grazed the skin with his soft mouth when they both jumped.

"Help, please! Someone help me!" a woman's voice was screaming. "Melissa, where'd you go?" Sobbing followed the voice as it moved quickly toward the back of the flower gardens.

The dogs' ears immediately perked up, and they stood ready to obey orders.

Nelly looked around but couldn't determine exactly where the cry for help was coming from.

"Rogue, Spike, Zook." Nelly gave the German command for search or track. Since they were already aware of a call for help, all she had to do was let them off their leash and they began their search.

With their ears, it was easy for them to pinpoint exactly where the woman was. Nelly and Mick followed closely, and when the two dogs found the anxious woman turning around in circles, they stopped and sat looking at her.

Nelly put the leashes back on and patted both heads. "Braver Hund." They deserved her praise.

Mick stopped the woman from her stunned circling and put both hands on her shoulders. Looking into her eyes, he gave her a small smile, the kind that he used to give her whenever she was stressed about a dog, or a test. "Ma'am, what's wrong?"

Crazy eyes looked at Mick, then all over. "My baby, she's gone."

"How old is she?" Cody asked.

Nelly was so focused on the woman, she hadn't heard anyone coming. But she should have noticed when both Rogue and Spike turned their heads before Cody spoke. They had heard his approach, but knew him well enough to not worry.

The woman looked at Cody for a second and then her crazed gaze looked all around at nothing, or no one. "She's six. She's got a pretty pink, flowery dress on. Melissa was standing right next to me one second, then I turned to look at some flowers. When I turned back, she was gone. I called out, but she won't come back to me." Tears streaked down her cheek.

"Ma'am, do you have anything with her scent on it?" The dogs could track a person, but they weren't very experienced in following a stranger's scent. However, it was one of the commands Nelly had trained them for.

"What? Oh, yes." The mother reached into her large bag and pulled out a rag doll. It would have Melissa's scent on it, but also the mother's.

Nelly took it and wafted it below each dog's nose. "Zook." Again, she let them off their leash and the dogs seemed to understand what they needed to do. Children were inherently precious to dogs. Especially these dogs. Boxers and Labrador Retrievers were both excellent with children. Even Spike, who didn't care too much for men, loved kids.

They sniffed the area and kept moving along, scenting the ground and the air. As they worked, they ignored the flowers. These dogs knew when to work and when to play. Smelling flowers was play time, and they knew the difference. Nelly was very proud of both of them. Nelly, Cody, Mick, and the mother all followed the dogs.

The mother tried to get in front, but Nelly stopped her. "Ma'am, the dogs are working, you'll need to stay back behind me and let them do their job."

"But, it's my baby out there." She turned sad eyes to Cody, who took her in his strong arms.

"Ma'am, what's your name?" Cody spent some time trying to keep the woman's mind occupied with other things all while they followed the dogs. Turned out her name was Martha.

As the group tracked the missing girl, other patrons and staff noticed them, and they had a line of people asking all sorts of questions.

Nelly turned back and asked, "Cody, can you take the mother and these people and have them spread out to look? I don't want anyone getting in the way of the dogs." She had another thought, but kept it to herself. She didn't want to worry Martha.

"Sure, thing. Good idea." Cody took the rest and had them stop as he told them the story and assigned various spots on the farm to look.

Mick followed Nelly. "Do you think it's wise to set them all off on their own? Aren't there bears and other wild animals around here?"

A soft snort escaped Nelly's nose. "There is, but with all of the people on the farm lately, I doubt any wild animals are nearby. Humans tend to scare away most animals."

"But, what about the bears?" Mick looked nervously around, and got so close to Nelly, that he almost tripped her up.

"Watch it." She glared at him. "You're just fine. The bears in this neck of the woods are just as afraid of you as you are of them. Stay clear of their cubs and you won't have any issues." The thought of the local honeybees that were used to pollinate the flowers came to her mind, but she shrugged that off. The bees were kept in their hives at the back of the fields. If they did attract the bears, she doubted any would still be out. With the sun setting, most bears would be back close to their own caves, or wherever they bunked down for the night.

"If you say so." Mick didn't sound convinced. In fact, he sounded more like a scaredy cat than a full-grown man.

Mick was no better than a regency era dandy. And to think, she had at one time thought he was quite the man. But, she couldn't be too hard on him-he was a city boy, after all. And those who lived in Montana were used to wild animals, while those who lived in Atlanta had only seen animals in the zoo.

They continued through the flowers until they came to the end, by the tulips. The dogs stopped and looked back at Nelly, then moved slowly forward. Nelly listened intently when both dogs bared their teeth and snarled.

Not too far away was the sound of a little girl crying. Nelly's heart just about broke. The poor thing probably chased a butterfly, only to get lost and not know how to find her way back.

"Why are the dogs snarling?" The worry in Mick's voice stopped Nelly in her tracks.

The dogs did that at times, especially when there was a man nearby that they sensed had bad intentions. Could Melissa have been taken by a bad man?

The dogs stopped at the edge of the flowers and continued to growl. It was a deep, guttural sound that they normally only used when real danger was near.

The hairs on the back of Nelly's neck stood on end. While she didn't know what danger awaited them, she knew something was wrong. "Melissa? Is that you?"

"Help!" the strained voice of a little girl called out.

The dogs growled, then barked, but they stood their ground, waiting for a command.

"Geh Raus." The command for go ahead came without any forethought. Nelly knew the little girl was in danger, and she hoped they weren't too late.

"Wait." Mick held her shoulder. "Let the dogs check it out first."

Nelly jerked her shoulder away. "No. I need to go and help that little girl. You can stay here if you want, but she's in danger, or hurt." She started forward.

It was a few steps before she heard Mick grumble something unintelligible under his breath, and then he followed her.

Trees lined the space between the flowers and the forest beyond the property. There was a wooden fence, but the slats had fallen down, almost as though someone had taken them out of the post and laid them there.

When the dogs jumped in front of the little blonde girl who was on the ground nursing a bloody knee, Nelly's heart stopped.

# Chapter 22

Right in front of the girl, with teeth bared and saliva dripping from its giant maw, was a mountain lion. Nelly hurried to the girl's side and picked her up. The dogs kept close by. "Pass Auf," she commanded the dogs to guard, but not to attack. The last thing she needed was a fight in front of this scared little girl.

Nelly was pretty confident her dogs would win, but she didn't want them to get hurt, and she certainly didn't want the little girl to see such violence.

The mountain lion was brown and white and growled his displeasure at the disturbance of his almost meal. She knew that little kids were sometimes eaten by mountain lions, but to have it almost happen right here, at the tree farm, was too much.

"Tell the dogs to attack and let's get out of here." Mick pulled on her arm, but stayed behind her and let her be the shield against the wild animal.

Nelly shook her head. "Are you crazy? Not in front of the little girl. Besides, if we can get out of this without hurting the animals, then we should."

"That... that... lion was about to pounce on the girl and eat her alive. It needs to be put down." Of course a city boy would think such a thing.

"No, Mick. We just need to get out of its way. I highly doubt that it'll chase us back to the main part of the farm. It probably wouldn't even pass the fence line if the posts weren't down." Part of Nelly wanted to make Mick put the fence posts back up, but with the mountain lion just about ready to pounce, she knew that would be foolish. "Let's back away and the dogs will come with us. They'll keep the mountain lion from following."

All three animals continued to snarl and glare at each other.

Once Nelly and Mick were a few feet back, with Melissa still in Nelly's arms, she called for the dogs to keep guard, and follow them back.

With the threat there, the dogs walked slowly backwards and kept their eyes on the wild animal. It didn't move, but it did keep his eyes on all of them.

When the dogs stopped their growling, Nelly figured they were far enough away from the mountain lion that it was safe to turn around and head quickly back to the crowds. Cody would need to send some men out here with guns, and a work crew to ensure that the fence was fixed quickly, and that the mountain lion stayed away.

When they were within shouting distance, Mick called out for help. A group of men came running and looked at them expectantly.

"There's a dangerous wild animal back there." Mick pointed to where they had come from. "You better get some guns and go after it. The thing just about ate the little girl."

"Mick!" Nelly admonished. She nodded to the mother, and then glared at him.

"What? They need to get out there and shoot the thing. If we hadn't shown up when we did, this little girl would have been lion food."

Martha screamed and ran to her daughter. "Melissa! Did the lion bite you? Are you alright?" She didn't give her daughter a chance to say anything before she noted the bloody knee. "Oh my goodness! Did it hurt you? You're bleeding."

Melissa had quieted down by the time they reached the other end of the flower beds. But now, with her mom freaking out, fear crossed her face and she began to wail. The little girl reached her arms out for her mother and almost fell out of Nelly's grasp.

"She's fine, just a scraped knee. A little antibiotic ointment and a Band-Aid will fix her up fine." Nelly gratefully handed the crying girl to her mom.

Without a word, Martha took her daughter and practically ran to the ranch house, even though it wasn't open to visitors. Old Mr. Makinaw was at the back door and welcomed them inside.

Remembering her one encounter with Joseph, Nelly prayed that the old man had his false teeth in. Seeing a toothless old man was enough to scare a kid at the best of times, let alone when the little girl was already frightened halfway out of her mind. He was a sweet old man, but a toothless old man even gave her the shivers.

Once they were inside the house, Cody and Daniel turned to Mick. Cody asked, "What was the animal, and how close did it get to the little girl?"

"It almost ate her," Mick said. "The ferocious beast was about to pounce on her when we showed up. It was a good thing I was there. I think I scared it away." He puffed out his chest and tried to take all the credit.

Spike chuffed at Cody, and then turned to look at Mick and growled. Her dogs were smart.

Nelly rolled her eyes heavenward. "Come on, I'll show you where we found them. And it was the dogs that stopped the mountain lion from attacking, not a human." She glared at Mick. "You might want to stay here, and check your pants." A tiny smile tugged at the edges of her lips. It would serve Mick right if he had peed his pants.

Sam ran up to them. "Are you alright? What happened?" He ignored Mick and patted Rogue and Spike on their heads. "Braver Hund."

Nelly was surprised to hear Sam tell them they were good dogs. She didn't realize he'd picked up any of the commands. And when both dogs licked his hand, she about died from shock. That was the first time Spike had shown any sort of affection for Sam. Sure, Spike had stopped growling at the cowboy recently. In fact, he'd stopped growling the day Mick showed up. How strange was that?

"I'm gonna go get the shotguns." Cody looked to Daniel. "You go get the equipment to fix the fence. We'll meet back here and all head out together."

"Right, and I'll let Javier know to close down the back section of the flower fields." Daniel nodded and left to get the supplies.

Not ten minutes later they were all gathered near the edge of the snapdragons.

"I'll have the dogs lead, just in case. Cody, you and Daniel should be right behind me with your guns ready." Nelly started forward, but Sam stopped her with his right hand on her shoulder.

"Wait, let me go first." Sam put himself between Nelly and the dogs.

Nelly's heart softened to the gruff cowboy, and she caught herself before she sighed. Now wasn't the time to swoon over a sexy man trying to protect her. They needed to ensure the mountain lion was far away, and the fence was fixed. "Actually, since they're my dogs, I need to be out front. But you can walk beside me."

Quietly, more than ten men, Nelly, and her two dogs made their way through the field of flowers. When they got close, the dogs began to growl again.

"Halt." Thankfully, the English command for stop was the same word as the German. It made it easier for all in the hunting party to know what she wanted, which included the dogs. "This is just about the place we found Melissa."

Cody and Daniel moved forward.

"Will the dogs accept us moving in front of them?" Cody asked.

"Yes, they will." Nelly looked to the dogs and commanded, "Steh." The dogs took up a protective stance in front of her and didn't move. They did keep growling and snarling their displeasure, though.

She and Sam moved to the front and looked around to see what had the dogs on edge. The hair on the back of Nelly's neck stood on end and she felt eyes on her. And not the ones of the men behind her, either. Something was out there.

Rogue's growling got louder, and Spike wouldn't let his friend outdo him, so he growled even louder.

As Nelly looked to her right, Sam looked to the left. Then something caught his attention - a rustle or a growl? He moved closer to Nelly, and the second he saw what was coming, he pushed her down to the ground and put up his left arm to block his body.

Rogue didn't wait for his command; he also jumped into the fray, with Spike only a step behind him.

The mountain lion let out a raspy growl that sent shivers down Nelly's spine, but she got up quickly when she heard Sam's grunt.

The wild animal had his sharp teeth sunk into Sam's left arm. He hit the beast on the head, trying to dislodge it from his body.

Rogue's teeth latched onto the mountain lion's hindquarter while Spike caught a front paw. Together, they yanked the animal off of Sam.

Sam fell back, teetered a bit, but righted himself before he could fall over.

Behind them, Cody and Daniel ran up and aimed their guns at the mountain lion the moment it was clear of Sam and Nelly. In unison, as though they had practiced this very thing for years, they shot at the lion's body. It fell down with one paw twitching before all movement ceased.

"What the...?" one man in the party exclaimed.

"Sam, are you alright?" Nelly ran to his side and took his left arm in her hands. For a moment, she had forgotten his left arm was a prosthetic. She almost asked why there wasn't any blood, then caught herself. "Did it hurt you?"

Sam rolled his sleeve up and took off his glove. "Well, I'd say it's toast. I doubt those gouges can be fixed." The lion had left large teeth marks in his arm. He grimaced and put his arm down.

"I'm so sorry, Sam. But thank you for getting between me and the lion." Fear infused Nelly as she thought about what might have happened to her arm if the animal had gotten her instead.

Rogue rubbed up against Sam's leg and chuffed to get his attention.

Sam leaned down and rubbed the dog's head with his right hand. "Braver Hund. Good dog." He leaned down and hugged the boxer. "Thank you for helping me. You're a very brave dog."

Spike was next to Nelly and she leaned down to give him a hug and rubbed the top of his head. "Good dog. I'm proud of you, Spike." She turned her head to look at Rogue. "And you, too, Rogue. Good dog. Tonight, you'll both get extra treats."

The dogs knew that word, and both barked their excitement.

Spike licked Nelly's face while Rogue did the same to Sam.

"I think you've got a new best friend." Nelly smiled and knew that Sam was going to be paired up with Rogue. There was no doubt as to what Rogue wanted, and the way Sam was grinning from ear to ear, Nelly knew Sam was finally in agreement.

"Do you think Spike will want me instead?" Sam looked to Spike and winked.

# Chapter 23

"Sam, I'm so sorry. I don't know how that fence was knocked down." Cody paced the kitchen as Sam looked over his prosthetic arm.

"Don't worry about it. I'd bet it was neighbor kids just having some fun. But you might want to put up some signs discouraging that sort of behaviour." Sam scowled at his arm.

"Again, Sam. I can't thank you enough for stepping between me and that mountain lion. That was either really brave or stupid." Nelly bit her lower lip and furrowed her brows. She couldn't get a good look at Sam's arm because he had his back to her.

Every time she moved around in an attempt to see it, he moved so that she couldn't see it. Nelly knew he was self-conscious. But she didn't care that he was missing an arm. In fact, it turned out to be a Godsend that he had a hard plastic arm. That was what saved them both from those ferocious teeth. However, she wasn't sure she should say it.

Mick on the other hand, was seriously lacking tact. "Wow, man. That's crazy. You've got a fake arm? It's a good thing. Otherwise, it would have hurt when the lion attacked." He walked closer, trying to get a look at it.

Rogue growled at Mick. Which was a first, that Nelly knew of.

"Rogue, Fuss." Part of Nelly was embarrassed that Rogue would growl at Mick, and part of her was glad. The dog would be a perfect companion for Sam.

Rogue obeyed, but he stepped closer to Sam and gave a dog's version of a menacing look at Mick. He showed his teeth and glared before turning his attention, and love, onto Sam.

Nelly had to put her hand over her mouth to keep her smile a secret.

Spike stuck close to Nelly. She understood. The room was full of men, and since Spike wasn't a fan of adult men, Nelly would be happy to have the dog close on her heals. She put a hand on Spike's head and rubbed it. Spike leaned his head against her leg and she understood he was trying to convey his love for her.

"Sam, I know it's going to be expensive, but let me pay for the replacement arm. It's the least I can do for you. You saved everyone today." Cody held out his hands in a pleading gesture.

Mick rolled his eyes, but stayed quiet.

Nelly would have slapped him upside the head if he'd made one more rude comment. As it was, she needed to get him out of there and away from Sam. The last thing Sam needed was negativity. She knew him well enough to know that he was going to be extra hard on himself, now that this group had seen his weakness.

Not to mention the way the men in the hunting party looked at him when they all saw his damaged arm. She grimaced when she remembered not only the shock, but also horror on two men's faces.

"Sam, would you like to keep Rogue today? I need to get Spike back." She frowned at Mick. "And Mick. Then I'll come over to the Crooked Arrow and we can talk."

Keeping his arm away from Nelly's eyes, he looked down at Rogue. The dog was sitting at his feet and had an expression of love and longing. Even if Nelly wanted to take Rogue with her, she doubted he'd be happy about leaving Sam.

"I don't think I should." Sam turned to look out the window. There were still a lot of people milling about, even though the flower show was over for the day. The sun had already set and the night sky was vibrant with the stars shining down on the Earth.

Nelly called Rogue to her side, but the dog just sat there looking up at Sam, expectantly. "Well, I don't know if you have a choice. Rogue doesn't seem to want to leave your side."

Sam's shoulders visibly relaxed when he looked down at Rogue. Then he used his only good hand and pat the dog's head. "Good dog. Do you want to stay with me?"

Rogue chuffed his agreement and licked Sam's hand.

"Well, there you have it. I'll be by the ranch later to bring some dog food and we can talk. I think Rogue is going to want to stay the night with you, if you don't mind? I can bring a doggie bed for him to use if you don't mind him sleeping in your room? Or I can bring a kennel so he can stay in the barn." Nelly hoped and prayed that Sam would take the dog and want him to sleep in his room with him. She didn't expect that Sam would want an eighty-pound dog in his bed.

"Why would Rogue want to stay with Sam? I don't get it?" Mick looked between Sam and Nelly, then down to Rogue. His brows furrowed and he really did seem confused.

Nelly sighed. "I'll explain it on the way back to my ranch. And Sam, I'll call before I come over. Just let me know what you or Jerod want me to bring." She knew Jerod would be totally fine with the dog, it was the plan all along to pair up dogs with vets who needed one.

Nelly said her goodbyes and told Mick to follow her out to his SUV. As they walked, she stayed a few paces ahead of him and had Spike between them for an added buffer. She knew she needed time to cool her jets.

Back in Atlanta, Mick had always seemed to say the right things, do the right things, and was just all around pleasant. Well, except for the end. But that was to be expected, right? When a couple is headed for a breakup things go wrong.

At first, she wasn't happy to see Mick. Then she was happy, then confused. Now, she was mad. How was it that Mick could be so rude? Or was it that he was just uninformed? Maybe he didn't realize his actions and words were inappropriate and downright rude? She should probably let her anger go and inform him that he was out of line. But do it nicely.

When they were all inside the SUV and Mick had pulled away from the Big Sky Farm, he turned his head toward Nelly and tried to smile. When she ignored him, he reached his hand across the distance and took her hand.

But she pulled it back.

"You're mad. I can tell. What did I do? Should I have been the one to jump in between you and the lion?" Mick had turned his eyes back on the road and was headed to her ranch as fast as the speed limit allowed.

"No, Mick. This has nothing to do with the mountain lion. Which by the way, is different from a lion." She ran a hand down her weary face. "You were rude and out of line with Sam. Yes, he had a prosthetic arm. But you shouldn't have said anything about it. Only those who are friends with him can talk about it. And the way you acted." She sighed. "You have no clue how to be around wounded vets, do you?"

They drove along in silence for a few minutes before Mick answered, "I'm sorry. If you want, I'll go back and apologize to Sam. And you're right. I've never interacted with a wounded vet before. And I've certainly never seen a fake arm up close. I think I've only seen it on TV. Honestly, I didn't mean anything by it."

She sighed. "I know, Mick. But this is my career. I will always interact with wounded vets. Some will have visible signs of their disability, while others won't. But anyone who gets one of my dogs will have a need. A need that needs to be treated with kindness and respect. No pity can ever show up in your voice, or face."

Wordlessly, Mick nodded his understanding. Nothing else was said until they were back at the barn. When they got out and Nelly had put Spike away, Mick too her hand. "What does this mean for us?"

"It means I'm right where I need to be, Mick." Nelly put her free hand to his cheek. "I will always choose to work with veterans. That's my calling and my passion."

"I know. It's because of your brother, right?" He squeezed her hand.

Nelly nodded. "I do care for you, Mick."

"But not enough to give this up for me." It wasn't a question, Mick knew the truth.

"Well, do you love me enough to give up your car dealerships and move here to be with me?" Nelly had always wondered why society expected the woman to be the one who uprooted her life and gave up on her dreams and aspirations to become some man's wife. It wasn't that she was a bra-burning, card-carrying member of the women's rights movement. But she did think that if two people were meant to be together, then they'd work out the logistics together. No man who wanted her should expect her to give up her passion, without even discussing it with her.

In time she might choose to move away. But right now, she knew she was in the right place. The day's events had proven it. Watching how Rogue protected Sam, and then helped to calm him down without even being asked or commanded to do so, told Nelly those two were meant to be together.

If she hadn't come to town, then Sam would never have met his perfect companion. And

Rogue was Sam's perfect companion. He may not realize it yet, but we have on his way to recognizing the bond he already shared with Rogue.

Without a word, Mick pulled her into an embrace. When he pulled away from her, she could see the sadness in his eyes, and his decision to leave.

*Chapter 24*

S am watched as Nelly and Mick walked away, with Spike between them. He wasn't sure, but he thought there might be trouble in paradise. Did that mean she was going to turn Mick down? Would the pretty dog trainer be staying in Frenchtown?

Rogue rubbed against his leg to get Sam's attention. "Yes, boy. I'm glad you're staying the night with me." Sam smiled down at his companion and wondered for the first time what it might be like to have Rogue stay with him forever.

Nelly was lending Rogue to him for the night. He knew that much for sure. Sam was also grateful. The dog seemed to calm him down. At first, when the mountain lion latched onto his arm, his first thought was grateful to have that fake arm. But then, once those men looked at him the way they did, shame filled him once more. He could feel himself begin to spiral down into his own private pit of despair.

Until Rogue nudged his leg.

Once the dogs were clear of the dead animal, Rogue instantly found him and checked on him.

There wasn't any pity in the dogs face, only love and concern. While Sam wasn't a dog whisperer, or anything, he could swear Rogue was sending him love and only wanted to help him feel better.

And it worked. He avoided his usual pit and his mind cleared. At least until Mick began, then he started to see red. Again, Rogue lent him his warmth and without a word brought Sam back up to Earth, and away from his usual pitfalls.

He didn't understand how a dog could do so much for him, but Rogue knew what he needed. And the dog not only gave him unconditional love, he tried to protect him. In fact, both dogs worked together to get the mountain lion off his arm.

Which shocked him. Spike had never shown much interest in Sam. Nelly had done a fantastic job training these dogs. They didn't even hesitate to jump in and protect. Sam had never thought of himself as a dog person, but he was starting to think he might be.

"Sam, how can I help?" Cody was still worrying about his arm.

"Cody, don't worry. It will be fine. I'll call the VA on Monday and they'll get me a new one if they can't fix this one. It wasn't like we were out partying and messing around."

"Well, if they charge you anything at all, you let me know. I can't even begin to tell you how grateful I am that you helped save that little girl. And you protected Nelly. You didn't even think, you just jumped in front of the mountain lion as it went to pounce on Nelly. You're a hero." Cody's enthusiasm was too much for Sam.

He shook his head. Sam wasn't a hero, and everyone in his unit knew it. He got lucky. Well, he was lucky today. After everything that went down in Afghanistan, he knew he was unlucky. So today's turn of luck must have been the universe setting things right. It still had a long way to go, but at least he was finally starting to see a benefit. "No, I'm not a hero. Those dogs, they're the heroes."

Sam smiled down at Rogue, who's tongue lolled to the side. "Braver hund." He scratched Rogue's head and then pet the dog's back. He'd have to see if the butcher in town had any bones the dogs could have. He wanted to pay them back for their bravery and support.

As Sam turned to head back to the Crooked Arrow, Cody again offered to pay him and of course Sam declined. Cody was a good man, and Sam was starting to warm up to the nice cowboy, and his fiancé, Sadie.

When he arrived back at the Crooked Arrow, thanks to a ride from Daniel Caruthers, he was grateful. The foreman of the Big Sky Farm never looked at him with pity. He also didn't treat Sam any different from other men. Daniel was a fair man, and was just as happy as he was to ride in silence back to the farm.

The only thing Daniel said was thanks for helping with the wild cat situation. Which was exactly they way Sam wanted it, he helped. He wasn't the hero and he didn't deserve any recognition. There was no way he could have done it on his own. Taking down the mountain lion was a team effort.

When he walked inside, Jerod, Dana, and the whole house was waiting for him. It seemed the rumor mill was alive and well in Frenchtown.

"Oh, thank goodness." Dana hurried over to him and pulled him into a giant hug. While they were friends, he had never hugged the woman. Well, he did on her wedding day, but wasn't that expected?

"Dana, I'm fine. Really, I am." Sam pulled back and gave her a lopsided smile.

Jerod put a hand on his shoulder. "Thanks for stepping up over there. It's all over town already how much you helped."

Sam should have known Jerod would know exactly what to say, while still conveying the fact that the town was going to go bonkers over him. He would stick close to the Crooked Arrow for the next few days, or until a new bit of juicy gossip took over the wagging tongues.

"Did you also hear about Rogue staying here?" Sam's eyes moved down to the canine companion sitting quietly at his feet. Rogue had spent enough time around all the guys from the Crooked Arrow this past week, since they'd all been over at Nelly's place. Nelly had brought the dogs around them all. It wasn't just part of their training, but also so they could get acquainted with the vets.

"Hey, buddy." Jerod squatted down and grinned at Rogue before putting his hand out for the dog to sniff.

Rogue still had his working vest on, so all the men knew to keep their distance unless invited to come close. Even though Jerod wasn't invited, he still was a little bit cautious and didn't go right in for the petting.

"Oh, right. I should probably take his vest off." Sam leaned down and released the clasps holding the vest in place.

The moment the vest was off, Rogue knew he was on his own time. The dog nudged his head under Jerod's hand and expectantly waited for the welcomed pets and scratches that the dog knew was forthcoming.

All of the guys, as well as Dana and Megan, came over and spoke to the dog as though he was a new resident at the ranch, and not an overnight guest.

Before everyone was finished with their hello's to the dog would lapped up their attention, Sam's cell phone rang. "Hello?" He hadn't bothered to check the screen to see who was calling, he was too focused on Rogue. For just a moment he worried that it would be a telemarketer, and breathed a sigh of relief when he heard her familiar voice.

"Hey, Sam. How's Rogue?" Of course Nelly's first concern would be her dog.

Sam grinned when he watched Rogue licking Skeeter's face. "Oh, I'd say Rogue is doing better than anyone else."

A soft, lilting laugh came over the phone and it filled him with warmth. "That's good to know. How are you doing?"

"You know me, no complaints." Which really meant that Sam had a lot of complaints but he just wasn't going to list them over the phone.

"How about I come over now with Rogue's things and we can talk about how to help him settle in for the night?" Nelly waited for his response.

"Sure." Sam wasn't sure if he was ready to see her with Mick again. "Will your boyfriend be joining you?"

"No." She was a bit short in her response.

Sam wondered if his question was rude or if she was mad at the city slicker. He hoped it was the latter. "Okay, see you soon."

It took Nelly almost an hour to get there, but when she did, he realized that he had been looking forward to seeing her again. Something he shouldn't have felt. She had a boyfriend. And Sam was anything but boyfriend material. He knew he should be happy for her, but that Mick wasn't right for her. Nelly needed a cowboy.

Sam answered the door when it rang and his stomach began doing somersaults. Nelly stood there in blue jeans, boots, and a short sleeved button up light blue blouse that set off her tan in a way that made his somersaults multiply.

"So, do you need any help getting Rogue's overnight gear out of the truck?" Sam stepped outside onto the porch with Rogue at his heals. He expected the dog to run to the truck, or at least to stand next to Nelly, but he didn't. The dog stayed right next to him.

Sam noticed that Nelly had pursed her lips, but her eyes sparkled and crinkled around the outer edges. Was she trying to hold back a smile, or a laugh?

After Nelly cleared her throat, she leaned down and scratched underneath Rogues head. "Good boy. Do you like it here?"

It surprised Sam when Rogue nodded as though he understood what she was asking. He was probably just nodding his enjoyment of her attention.

"Of course, you do. Braver Hund." She leaned in and hugged the dog. Then she ran her hands down his back.

Images of Nelly wrapping her arms around him and running her fingers down his back sent shivers through his entire body. He had to get those sorts of thoughts out of his mind. He was never going to have her like that.

Morose thoughts ran through Sam's mind, and he blurted his question before he could even catch himself. "So, where's the rich boy."

All of a sudden, pressure so intense Sam thought he might explode, enveloped him. He winced and held his breath as he waited for her reply.

Nelly stood up and pursed her lips. This time, her eyes didn't sparkle or crinkle. "He went home."

"You mean back to his hotel?"

"No, I mean back to Atlanta."

A slow smile spread across his face and all of the pressure he had felt since asking Nelly about the guy broke and lightness took over. Even though the sun had set, all Sam saw was sunshine and possibilities.

"So, does mean..." Before he could finish his question Nelly interrupted.

"He's not coming back. I'm so sorry about how he treated you earlier. I've never seen him act like this before. But then again, he's never been around anyone but rich people."

"And pretty people, I imagine." Sam knew before he lost his arm he was handsome, but he could never be described as a pretty boy. Sam had a rugged look to him. And now with his arm, well. Like he had said may times, he would never be considered pretty, or handsome anymore.

Nelly let a light chuckle escape before she straightened and stood up. "He had no right to say anything like that and I'm sorry."

Sam waved her off. "Don't worry. It was nothing new."

Nelly worried at her lower lip and tilted her head. She looked as though she was thinking about something and didn't know what to say.

In that very moment, Sam's heart stopped and all he could think of was taking her lips in his. But he couldn't. Could he? Without any forethought, he jumped off the cliff and went for it. "Nelly, have dinner with me?"

Her eyes widened and one side of her mouth slid up in a half smile. "Okay."

Sam blinked. Had he really asked her out? What was he thinking? He couldn't do this. She deserved so much better. He felt his pulse increasing and his breathing labored. But before he could start to hyperventilate, Rogue chuffed and rubbed his head against Sam's leg. "Rogue, do you approve?" He hoped he did. In fact, Sam just might have to take the dog with him. All it took was the dog getting his attention and he was able to stop himself from falling into his pit, again.

Nelly rubbed the dog's head. "Of course, he does. When do you want to go out?"

When he asked her out, he hadn't thought of anything other than an opportunity to kiss her. But that couldn't be their date. He had to take her out to dinner or something like that. "How about

Wednesday night?" Since it was Saturday evening, that should give him time to wrap his head around what he had just done.

"Why not tomorrow night?"

Sam sucked in a breath and put his hand on the top of Rogue's head. He needed the strength the dog offered him. This was going too fast. If he was completely honest with himself, he would have probably found a way to get out of the date before Wednesday. But tomorrow night? He had no idea how he could get out of it so quickly.

"Ah, yeah. Sure." What else could he say? It wasn't like he could say he had to wash his hair. That was one of those excuses one girl had used when he was in high school. At first, he thought it really did take the whole night for women to wash their hair. Then he asked his mom about it and learned the truth.

# Chapter 25

What was she thinking? She should have never accepted his offer. But how could she say no to him? He looked so hopeful and cute asking her out. Nelly shook her head as she drove home later that night. She had gotten Rogue and Sam all situated for the night, and if she was being honest with herself, forever.

Nelly doubted that Rogue would be coming back to her, unless it was to visit. The dog had already bonded with the man. And the man, while he didn't know it yet, had also bonded with the dog. She noticed that he had reached out to touch Rogue a few times when he was obviously nervous.

Some might thing she agreed to go out with him for the wrong reasons. Some might even think it was a pity date. But it wasn't. Nelly really liked Sam. Before Mick showed up, she thought they were heading in this direction. Although, she didn't think he'd ask her out so quickly. And she certainly didn't think she'd be so bold as to suggest they go out the very next night. "Where did that come from?"

Nelly looked around and realized she was talking to herself, out loud. "I think I'm going nuts." It was a good thing she was driving down a deserted road, no one was able to see her silliness. Although, she thought she remembered reading somewhere that those who spoke to themselves had a higher IQ. She'd go with that.

The next morning she wondered how the rest of her dogs would handle not having Rogue around. When Nelly went to the stalls that she used as kennels, she noticed that Spike was looking around and sniffling through the straw on the ground. She'd probably have to bring them all over to the Crooked Arrow that afternoon so they could see Rogue in his new home.

Or, maybe she should wait until Sam recognized that Rogue was home? She couldn't just leave the dog there and not have the conversation with Sam. He had to sign paperwork and everything to adopt his service dog. Then she'd have to file the paperwork with the VA and the national service dog registry. All paperwork required Sam to sign for Rogue.

While Spike didn't like men, he did like Rogue, a male Boxer. Spike tilted his black and white head and gave her a pleading look.

"I know, Spikey, you'll see Rogue again." Nelly noticed that Spike's whole body shook when she mentioned Rogue. The two of them were buddies. She might have to work to find Spike a human soon. But, there weren't any women at the Crooked Arrow yet. She knew there were two slated to arrive soon, but she didn't know when they would arrive. "Do you want to go and see Rogue now?"

A little chuff escaped the dog. The other two just looked at her and Spike then turned toward their water dishes. It was time to feed them and let them out for some exercise.

An hour late, Nelly and Spike were in her truck headed to church. She took turns taking them to church each week so they would get more time around crowds, and kids. Nelly and Sam hadn't discussed taking Rogue to church the next day, but she hoped Sam would have thought to do so. It would do Spike good to see his buddy with Sam. Another thought entered her mind and a slow smile crept across her face.

Rogue was at church with Sam and the dog sat on the pew next to Sam instead of lying on the ground as Nelly had trained them. She hoped the pastor didn't mind the dog being on the bench. She'd have to tell Sam that the dogs should sit or lay on the ground, not the church pews.

And of course, the moment Spike saw Rogue sitting on the bench, he had to climb onto the bench next to Nelly. Even though she didn't use the service dog vest today, she still used the German command to get down, "Platz." And Spike listened. He did move slowly down and had his tail between his legs, but he still moved to the ground where he knew he was supposed to sit or lay. At least Spike didn't bark or chuff.

Both dogs did great during the service and Nelly was proud of them. She couldn't help but feel like a mother to two young boys who spent their first

Sunday in the grown-ups church and were well behaved.

When church was over, Nelly took Spike and approached Sam and Rogue. "Well, I see that Rogue is settling in just fine." She gave the boxer a rub on his head.

Spike went to Sam and rubbed against his leg.

The shock was evident on Sam's face and he looked between Spike and Nelly.

"I think he recognizes that you're now partnered with Rogue and he's giving you his approval." Emotions filled Nelly's heart and she realized that she was going to miss Rogue. The cute boxer had so much personality, and he had really fit in well with her other dogs.

"Ah, thanks, buddy." Sam reached down and rubbed Spike's head and back.

Jerod and Dana joined them.

"So, has Rogue taken over the house yet?" Nelly asked.

Dana laughed. "Oh, I think he's now the ruler of the roost. All of the men had to pet Rogue this morning and a couple even smiled when they touched him. I think he's gonna have to stay with us now." She winked at Rogue. "Aren't you, boy?"

"Well, that is a possibility." Nelly turned her gaze on Sam. "Would you be willing to partner up with Rogue? It's a big responsibility, but I think he's already chosen you."

Sam's brows furrowed and he looked at the dog in the center of attention, then over to Spike who sat next to Nelly and looked at Sam expectantly. "Yes, I think I might. But what all is entailed?"

"How about we meet up and I can bring the paperwork. Then we can discuss the details further." If Nelly had been thinking properly, she would have brought it with her to church, but alas, she left it back at the barn.

With a grin, Dana suggested, "why don't you go home and get it. Then come over to the ranch for supper with us today? After we've eaten, you and Sam can go over the paperwork in the den."

That evening, after she had gotten all the paperwork completed and signed by Sam, Nelly enjoyed a cup of hot peppermint tea with Megan and Dana. "You know, I'm going to miss Rogue. But I'm glad he's found his partner."

"Is that how it works?" Dana took a sip of her piping hot tea. "Do the dogs do the choosing?"

"I always thought it was the trainers and psychologists who worked together to choose the human and dog who would best work together." Megan, who had already decided that Rogue would be a good match for Sam, waited for Nelly's reply.

"It can happen in various ways. No matter how they pair get together, the dog must accept the human, or it won't work. It's kinda like a marriage. In that both partners have to accept the other. Love will develop, but not a romantic love, obviously."

Dana and Megan giggled.

"Of course, not." Megan agreed. "But, what if the dog doesn't like the human you've chosen for him?"

"That wouldn't happen since I don't normally do the choosing. And if a dog didn't like who the counselor chose for him, then I wouldn't allow the match. Usually, a decision isn't made until the dog is comfortable with the human and vice versa. We have to watch them together for a while before we can know either partner will work well with the other." Nelly set her cut down on the table and picked up a madeleine cookie.

"Like how it naturally worked out with Sam and Rogue?" Dana asked.

"Sorta. Normally, it does go much faster. And to be honest, I never thought Sam needed a service dog. At first, I thought he was a ranch hand or maybe partners with Jerod in the ranch." Actually, Nelly hadn't thought too much about what Sam had been doing on the ranch when they first met. She had wondered, but didn't let the thought take root. Until she learned about Sam's prosthetic arm.

Dana nodded. "Have you seen any of the dogs take a special liking to any of the other guys here on the ranch?"

A slow smile crept across Nelly's face. "I have."

"Care to share a name?" Dana asked.

Nelly shook her head. "I don't think so. This is actually something that Megan needs to look into first."

Megan nodded. "Agreed. How about you bring the rest of the dogs over for visits next week? We can see how they interact with the men and determine if anyone is a good match."

"Most of them will be at my place all week working on the house." Nelly shivered just thinking about what was still left to sort through.

"I'll bring the dogs around the men and see if there is anyone who might do well with a dog. But Megan, you'll need to be there and observe as well."

By the time plans were finalized, Sam had entered the room and motioned for Nelly to join him. Once they were out of earshot, he reminded her of their date.

She grinned. "I hadn't forgotten. But with all the excitement of you adopting Rogue today, I wasn't sure if you might have forgotten."

Sam shook his head. "No, I'm just waiting for you to finish whatever..." he motioned to the room where the other women sat sipping their tea. "You were doing."

"Did you want to bring Rogue? Now that he's officially your service dog, you'll be able to take him anywhere you go, if you want." While Nelly wanted it to be just the two of them, she also knew she would have to work with Sam and Rogue in the public. They needed to both know what was acceptable behavior - and what wasn't.

Like sitting on the church pews.

"You want Rogue to join us for our date?" Confusion was evident as Sam furrowed his brows and tilted his head.

"While it may not be romantic, I do think that it would be good for me to be with you and Rogue when you go out. At least a few times. To make sure that you both understand your roles." Nelly knew that Rogue would be good, but training was needed no matter what.

While Sam did have a good, basic understanding of the German commands, he didn't know them all, and he also didn't know all of the rules and boundaries that needed to be in place.

The pregnant pause had Nelly a bit worried, but she needn't have.

"Okay. It's not like Jerod's going with us, or any other sort of chaperone, right?" Sam winced on the *chaperone* part.

A giddiness filled Nelly, but she kept herself from laughing, no matter how cute Sam was being. "Right. It will be just you, men, and Rogue."

"And the forty or so patrons at the diner." This time, Sam relaxed and grinned.

She returned his grin and made to say her goodbyes to everyone before joining Sam and Rogue in the Crooked Arrow truck.

"Okay, first order of business, when there is a back seat, you should have it covered with a blanket and make sure Rogue stays back there. He knows that's where he's supposed to be, but he will most likely try to climb into the front seat in the beginning." Since there wasn't a back seat to the truck, Nelly put a blanket down on the seat between her and Sam. "And if there is only a seat in the front, then this will do. Just be careful. We don't want Rogue to get hurt should you have an accident."

Nelly could tell the wheels were turning in Sam's head as he thought over all she had just said. "And if we use the van? Can I put him in the seat behind me? Or does he need to go further back?"

"The idea is to make sure Rogue's not in a position where he might fly through the windshield, or go too far forward, or backward, should there be an accident. So, in the van, I'd put him in the second row." Nelly did worry about her dogs, and she never wanted them to get hurt. So what if she was a bit overprotective sometimes.

Sam nodded his understand and ran a hand down Rogue's back.

The dog's tongue lolled out the side of his mouth and he looked forward, knowing that his two favorite people would be going somewhere. Rogue loved to go anywhere Nelly went, and she was sure that he would love going everywhere with Sam, too.

As they drove into Frenchtown, Nelly reflected on how it had only been a couple of days since she last came to town, with Mick. Tonight's date was very different from the one she had with her ex. This date gave her goosebumps and butterflies, but all for the right reasons. She was truly excited to be going out with Sam for their first date.

It was strange, too.

She'd only known the veteran for two weeks, and already she knew that she harbored exciting feelings for the man. Nelly was pretty sure Sam liked her, too, but she wasn't sure. Not yet. Although, a man rarely asked out a woman he didn't have romantic feelings for.

While Nelly had taken Rogue out to eat in restaurants, as well as her other dogs, this was a first for Sam. It would almost be like training a new dog on how to behave in a public place. Her lips twitched when that thought entered her mind.

"What?" Sam asked.

Nelly was taken out of her thoughts and turned wide eyes to Sam. "Huh? Sorry. I was thinking about the dogs." A rueful smile passed over her lips quickly and then she gave Sam her full attention.

"What about the dogs made you smile like that?" He tilted he head and looked closely at her.

"Oh, it's nothing. How about we get inside and see what there is to eat here?" Even though Nelly had been to the local diner a few times, she wanted to change the subject and was beginning to feel a bit nervous. She shouldn't have compared Sam to a dog, even if only in her mind. The last thing she needed was for him to discover what she was thinking. He'd never trust her again. And rightly so.

Nelly itched to grab the leash from Sam and take Rogue in herself, but she had to resist. This was Sam and Rogue's time to learn how to work together. Never mind that she was supposed to be on a date with the soldier.

"Is there anything special I need to tell Rogue as we enter the diner?" Sam looked over his shoulder to Nelly, who was two steps behind them.

"Nope. He knows what to do. But let me get the door, it will be easier if you two go in first." She walked to the door and opened it before Sam had a chance.

"Hey, this is supposed to be a date and I'm the one who should be opening doors, not you." One of his brows lifted up and he gave Nelly a half scowl.

She'd be happy if that was the only negative look he gave her all night, but she doubted it. "I know, and next time you can. But first get a feeling for how Rogue enters a building and let him get a feeling for you. Most strangers will open the door for you when they see the dog. You shouldn't be upset, let them do it."

"But, the man is supposed to open the door and let the woman enter first. It's just good manners." Sam may have been an old curmudgeon, but he was a gentleman.

Nelly was beginning to think she'd made a mistake in combining their date with training. It seemed like Sam really did want to make a good first impression with her. Something she really did appreciate. "Sam, our next date can be just the two of us. But, you do need to work with Rogue. Even if we weren't going to try dating, I'd still have to go out with you and Rogue and run through most of the normal scenarios with you two."

Sam stopped in the open door and glared at her. "Fine, but next date is going to be just the two of us and I'm going to be allowed to be a proper gentleman. Got it? I don't want to go out with a twenty-first century woman who can do everything for herself."

That caught her off-guard. "But, I am a modern woman with her own business. And I am very independent, thank you very much."

With a deep sigh, Sam let his shoulders droop. "That's not what I meant, and you know it."

"Fine, let's just go get a seat and we can talk about your caveman antics then." Nelly grinned to let him know she really didn't think he was a caveman. Let's be real, a caveman would have bonked her over the head and carried her over his shoulder to his cave. They wouldn't have even had this conversation. She knew he would have only grunted his disapproval and done what he wanted.

Sam was no caveman. He was a gentleman. And he wanted to prove that to her.

It was up to Nelly to let him show her his respect and appreciation for her.

# Chapter 26

S am knew that women in general could take care of themselves. Shoot, he'd been to war with plenty of women. He knew without a shadow of a doubt that women could take care of themselves in this day and age. And he had no problem with that. But his momma raised him to be a gentleman. And doggonit if he wasn't gonna try.

Once they were inside, he motioned for her to step in front of him and Rogue. Rogue was a male dog, he needed to learn how to be the canine version of a gentleman. His nose twitched and he did everything in his power to keep from smiling in that moment. The thought was his and his alone. Sam knew that if he smiled, Nelly would know something was up with him and she'd start asking him all sorts of questions.

Isn't that what women did whenever a man showed any emotion whatsoever on his face?

"How about I follow. I don't want Rogue to see me. He knows I'm here, but if I'm in his line of sight, he's gonna look to me for his queues. He must learn to read you, and not me." Nelly's reasoning did make sense. Didn't mean he had to like it, but he could understand.

The young waitress, Sam couldn't remember her name, but he'd seen her there several times in the past few months, pulled out two menus. "Two for dinner?"

"Yes, please. Come on, Rogue. Let's follow the waitress to our seat." Sam nodded to the teenager who took them to a table toward the back of the restaurant. He wasn't sure if it was because of the dog, or if that was just the next place to seat. The place was busy, and Sam understood that sections had to be filled up in a certain way so as to not overload a waitress.

However, there was a little voice telling him that the girl didn't want them to be seen and that was why they were being seated in the back. Sam hated it when the voice of doubt and low self-esteem asserted itself in his mind.

In the past, he would have let it eat him up and eventually he'd explode. But since he and Megan had begun working together, he recognized when it popped up and knew exactly what to think. Sam was much better than that voice wanted him to think. He reminded himself that he was worthy of sitting in the booth next to the window, if it wasn't already taken.

And if he was being honest with himself, a table was probably a better place to sit with the dog. And since it was their first time out together, he would probably do better out of the limelight. By the time they were seated and had their menus, that voice was gone.

In its place was contentment and the knowledge that he was worthy.

He was worthy to be out with Nelly.

He was worthy to be seen by everyone.

He was worthy to have Rogue by his side.

But most importantly, he was worthy of God's love.

Lately, reminding himself that God loved him usually put his frame of mind back where it belonged. Sometimes it took longer than he would have liked, but tonight he was doing alright. He'd only been thinking about God for about two weeks.

"So," Sam began once the waitress left them alone. "Can I feed Rogue anything from the menu?"

Nelly shook her head. "It's better to not feed him any table scraps, especially when you're out at a public place. Eventually, he'll come to expect it and he will start looking for your food instead of anything that might trip you up. Plus, the spices that cooks add to meat in restaurants isn't healthy for dogs."

"Wow, the dogs are always on duty, aren't they." It wasn't so much of a question, as it was Sam realizing how much Rogue was going to do for him. Not that Sam would let his guard down, it was ingrained him. And reinforced during war. But, knowing that Rogue was his battle buddy, of sorts, was going to make it all so much easier.

Unfortunately, he began to think about his last battle buddy, Henry. With the menu in front of him, he knew Nelly couldn't see the distress coming on. Whenever thoughts of Henry came on him, he had to work hard to calm himself down.

Under the table, Rogue began to whimper. Then he scooched closer to Sam and eventually put his head in Sam's lap.

Sam was making a concerted effort to get his breathing back under control, and bring his heart rate down. The last thing he needed was to have a panic attack while on a date. As he thought about Nelly, his hand reached down, and he rubbed Rogue's head. The action of petting the dog along with thinking about Nelly did the trick. Once he was under control, he put his menu down and realized that his semi-attack hadn't gone unnoticed.

"Want to talk about it?" It wasn't pity in Nelly's eyes, it was more the look of someone who understood and was there was for him. Her soft eyes beckoned to him and he did want to unburden. Just not here in a crowded restaurant.

After taking a shaky breath, Sam shook his head. "Not here."

She tilted her head and pursed her lips. Nelly's eyes narrowed and she looked from Sam to the side, where Rogue's body would be under the table. "Did he help?"

Sam almost scoffed at the idea, but then he remembered his hand was still on Rogue's head. "Yeah, I guess he did." He turned and smiled at the dog. "You're a good boy, aren't you? Braver Hund."

Rogue's tail wagged and he licked Sam's hand.

Which brought a short chuckle from Sam. "Yeah, I think he's gonna be great for me."

"And you are going to be great for him." Nelly nodded and smiled at Sam.

The waitress must have known they needed a moment, because as soon as Nelly smiled, the girl walked toward them and greeted them with a cheery grin and asked if they were ready.

Nelly watched as the waitress left them alone. "Sam, I think it might help if we talk about what just happened. I can't help you deal with the actual issue, that's what Megan does. But, what I can do is teach you how to use Rogue to help you. Luckily, you already have the instinct to reach out to Rogue."

"Yeah, how did he know I needed him?"

"This is why it's so important for the dog to bond with the human as well. He is becoming in tune with you and your body. He'll know before anyone else does if there's something wrong with you and he'll come to you. Dogs instinctively know when their human needs some loving and attention. Some dogs are trained to detect when their human is about to pass out, or even have a heart attack. It's amazing what dogs can sense before humans can. And they will bring either your attention to the issue, like he just did, or they will bring the attention of other people." Nelly beamed at Rogue, who had popped his head up and watched as she explained it all to Sam.

It was a lot to take in and Sam wasn't sure he understood it all. "So, you mean to tell me that Rogue will be able to sense when I'm about to spiral down into a pit of despair and he'll come and offer me comfort?"

Nelly put her elbows on the table and leaned forward, looking directly into Sam's eyes. "He will not only give you comfort and support, but the act of him coming to you and getting your attention will help to break up whatever is going on inside of you. When a person begins to have a panic attack, or as you said, spiral down into a pit of despair, all they need is a little nudge."

"A little nudge?"

"Did you feel Rogue pushing against your thigh?" Nelly asked.

He blinked a few times as he thought about what happened. Henry entered his mind and he whispered, "Henry."

Nelly sucked in a breath and her eyes began to water. "Henry? How did you know?"

Sam shook himself when he heard her voice, and at the same time Rogue nudged his thigh again. "What do you mean? Of course I know Henry."

Nelly jerked back in her chair. "It must be a different Henry. It's not a common name, but it's not Prince or Apple, either."

"Wait," Sam held up a hand. "I'm confused. Who is Henry to you?"

"Henry is my brother."

Sam's whole world began to crash down around him and the memories started to flood his mind. Henry had a younger sister. One who was studying to work with animals. But he'd never said she was going to train service dogs, did he?

All sound stopped and Sam's heart almost stopped with it. Then all he could hear was water rushing all around him as though he was going over the edge of a waterfall. Niagara Falls if the loud rushing sound was any indication. Breathing became difficult and he leaned over.

Under his hand he felt the comforting fir of a dog. Then sound began to return and he heard the dog bark. Then someone called his name from the distance.

Before he could get himself under control, he felt the sting of a slap across his face. "What?" His head jerked back and everything was a blur. Then *her* face came closer and started to come into focus. He mumbled, "Bumble Bee."

After that, it was all a blur until he sat in the passenger seat of his truck with a woman next to him crying and Rogue barking. His mind came back to him and he looked around. "What, where?"

"Nelly? What just happened?"

## *Chapter 27*

*I*t couldn't be. There was no way he was the same man. Nelly thought to herself. Her brother had written home many times about his buddy, but he had never actually said his name, had he? And when Henry came home all battered and bruised from the attack in Afghanistan, he did say that his partner had it worse than he did. Nelly's mind was a wash of confusion and questions. But Sam was in no condition to talk about it. She had to get him home and to Megan. She'd know exactly what to do.

They sat in the cab of the truck, with Rogue between them. The poor dog, he kept going back and forth between them both offering his comfort to each of them.

"It's alright, Rogue. Sam needs you more." Nelly kissed the top of the dog's head and turned him toward the man in the seat next to them. "Help Sam."

Rogue put his head up against Sam's chest and chuffed a few times to get his attention.

Nelly noticed when Sam was coming out of the memories because the man's eyes began to clear and she could tell he was focusing in her direction. "Sam? It's going to be alright. We're going back to the ranch."

She didn't want to drive until he was back with her and knew what was happening. Nelly had learned from experience with her brother it wasn't always safe to drive when a man suffering from PTSD went into a state of shock only to come out of it while she was driving. They almost crashed more than once when Henry thrashed around the cab of her truck.

Sam didn't reply, he just wrapped his arms around Rogue and nodded.

The drive back to the ranch was long and quiet. Nelly could hear Sam mumbling, but none of it made sense. She wanted to call Megan, but this wasn't her truck, so her phone wasn't connected. There was no way she was going to chance it and make a call without Bluetooth. All of her attention was needed on the road at the moment.

Memories of what her brother had told her in letters and after he came home started to come back. Tears streaked down her face as she thought about the man who had become her brother's best friend. When they had the funeral for her brother, her mother had told her that Henry's best friend was too injured to make the trip. She seemed to remember something about losing a limb, but she hadn't thought much about it, until now.

The clues had been there, but she had tried so hard not to think about her brother and his life, and death, since she arrived, that she missed them all. They had both been injured in a roadside bomb, but wasn't that practically a daily occurrence? Didn't most soldiers get hurt that way? But no, that wasn't really true. Yes, roadside bombs were quite common, but there were so many other ways soldiers were hurt and killed in the Middle East.

Her mind churned over all of the clues she had, but never thought about. But the one thing that didn't make sense was Sam's somber attitude. Her brother's best friend was a cheerful man. He played practical jokes and laughed a lot, if what her brother's letters reported was true. Sam? Not a joker and he rarely laughed. But the few times he had, she thought the action seemed right for Sam. He had laugh lines around his eyes.

If Sam hadn't used her brother's pet name for her, she wouldn't have believed it. Only her brother called her Bumble Bee. No one else, not even her parents did. That was their joke from when they were kids.

Nelly pulled into the drive leading up to the Crooked Arrow Ranch and noticed the sign and how it towered over the road. It was a simple sign of round posts that went up high and one large round post that tied to the ends together. On the middle of the large post was carved the words – Crooked Arrow Ranch. Nelly had never really thought much about the name before. But it made sense.

The drive wasn't exactly straight, it veered a little to the left and right. She noticed that there were larger boulders along the road that forced the road to turn. She would bet good money that from above it resembled a crooked arrow. Then, there was the Crooked Creek that ran behind the property.

They came to the house all too soon. Her mind was still a jumble of thoughts, none of them quite making sense. But they were there and Sam needed Megan. Without thought, her hand came down hard on the horn. She blasted it several times before Jerod came running out the door.

"What's wrong?" Jerod looked from her in the driver's seat to Sam in the passenger's seat. "Sam? Are you injured?" He went to Sam's side of the truck and opened the door. Rogue stayed right where he was until Sam took his hands off the dog.

"Sorry." Sam got out of the truck and walked into the house as though he was a zombie.

Rogue followed him but whimpered the whole way. He knew his buddy wasn't doing so well and was focused solely on the soldier. He didn't even look back at Nelly when they crossed the threshold.

"What happened? Why is Sam in a catatonic state?" Jerod closed the truck door and hesitated before turning to head back inside.

Nelly was right behind him. "He had an issue with a memory when we were at the diner. At first, he did great. So did Rogue. But then..." She sighed and ran a hand across her face to wipe a stray tear away.

"Then what?" Jerod asked.

"I think he was best friends with my brother." There, she had said it out loud. She never would have even thought I possible, even after he said her brother's name. But he called her bumble bee.

Jerod stopped and turned to Nelly. "Your brother was Henry? He...ah...he's no longer with us?"

A little gasp escaped her lips, and Nelly covered her mouth with one hand. More tears pooled in her eyes. The only thing she could do was nod.

Jerod pulled her to his side and gave her a tight hug. "Come on, I know where Sam is and I think we all need to be there for him, and for you."

Nelly followed Jerod as he led them down a long hall. When he stopped in front of a closed door, she could hear voices, but they were muffled. She furrowed her brow in confusion when Jerod knocked, then waited a couple of moments, and finally he opened the door.

What was inside surprised Nelly.

"Megan? Sam? Should we be here?" Nelly looked inside as Jerod walked in and took a seat across from Sam on a sofa. Megan sat in an overstuffed recliner, while Sam sat in a matching one next to her.

Megan looked up and nodded. A grim expression covered her pretty face. "Please, come in and join us. I think this session is one that you both need."

Not knowing what else to do, Nelly entered and closed the door behind her. When she took a seat on the sofa next to Jerod, she noted that Rogue was sitting on the ground next to Sam. "Braver Hund."

Rogue chuffed. He knew where he belonged, and what he was supposed to do.

Sam reached down and pat the dog's head. But his gaze was on her and it started to unnerve her a bit. "You're her, aren't you? Bumble Bee?"

A sudden sob rose and she put her hand over her face as began to cry. Nelly thought she'd never hear anyone call her Bumble Bee again.

Jerod put a hand on her arm and passed a box of tissue to her. After she thoroughly soiled at least one quarter of the box, she looked up and Sam was still watching her.

"You're the buddy Henry always wrote about." Nelly knew it was true.

"How did we not know?" Sam begged with his hands in front of him pleading for her to know the answers.

"He and I have the same last name. Didn't you ever wonder?" While Nelly may not have known the full name of her brother's friend, he had to know her last name.

Sam winced. "Honestly, I didn't really think about your last name. I mean, I knew it, I guess." He shrugged. "But I didn't think about it. And Henry made it sound like his little sister was going to school to become a veterinarian, not a dog trainer."

A snort escaped her. "Yeah, he said I should become a vet, instead of a trainer. He said I'd make more money that way." She never did it for the money. Nelly wanted to train dogs because it was her passion.

"Do you hate me?" Fear entered Sam's eyes and he hunched over, almost as though he was afraid she would hate him.

"Why would I hate you?" Nelly sniffled and used more tissue to clear up her crying.

"Because it was me who should have died, not Henry. He wasn't even injured as badly as I was. If I had died, he'd still be alive today." Tears began to streak down Sam's face.

Nelly heart ached for the poor man. She finally understood what made Sam so sad. "Sam, it's not your fault. If anything, it's mind." She put a hand to her chest. "I should have recognized the symptoms and got him the help he needed."

Megan interrupted. "You're both wrong. No one is to blame for Henry's death. He didn't die in battle, Sam. You weren't anywhere near him when it happened so there was nothing you could have done."

"But, he was my best friend. I should have been the one die, not him. He had so much more to live for then I did." Sam put his hands over his face, and Rogue whined before reaching his head up to nudge Sam's elbow.

The action caught Sam's attention and he brought his hands down. Using his left arm, he pet the dog. Sam's arm still wasn't fixed, and it wouldn't be for a while, but he still reached out with it, as though it was his own flesh and blood arm.

A tiny bit of hope entered Nelly's heart when she realized that Sam was in the process of healing. Even if it was just a tiny bit. Until that moment, she feared Sam might take the same path as her brother.

Nelly leaned forward. "Sam, I was the one who should have seen his symptoms. He carried so much hurt and anger in his heart when he came home. Henry always loved God and going to church when he was home, but someone the enemy got a foothold in his heart and worked to put up a shield between him and God. Henry was depressed and having a difficult time dealing with war. He was on meds, but it turned out to be the wrong ones." She stopped and had to wait as the sobs overtook her.

"Both of you are wrong," Megan interjected. "Henry committed suicide because he was on the wrong medication and his doctors didn't realize how bad his depression really was." She looked between the two of them. "If trained psychologists didn't recognize the symptoms, how could either of you done any different?"

"If I had died in that bombing, Henry wouldn't have been so upset. You should have seen him when he realized that I was going to lose my arm. He went off." Sam shivered with the memory.

"Sam, how do you think he would have felt if you'd have died? Do you really think he would have handled that better?" Megan asked.

Sam lifted his left arm. "All men know that a soldier isn't a man if he's lost a limb."

Nelly interrupted. "That's not true. Losing a limb doesn't make you less of a man. Your arm has nothing to do with your masculinity."

Sam jumped up. "Yes, it does! It has everything to do with what sort of man I am." He sank back down and put his head in hands as his shoulders shook with his tears.

Rogue put his head against Sam's legs.

Megan put a hand on his shoulder.

Nelly began to get up, but Jerod put a hand on her arm. "Wait."

"Sam, you know that your prosthetic doesn't make you less of a man. Nelly went out with you tonight knowing you lost your limb in war. It didn't her at all." Megan tried to sound soothing, but her words only set Sam off.

Sam's head jerked up. "You're wrong. She used our date to train me, like one of her dogs."

"I did no such thing!" Nelly jumped up and pointed at Sam. "I wanted to go out on that date with you. But I also knew that you needed time with me and Rogue both to help you. I'm sorry if I thought that training you and Rogue together on our first date was a bad idea, but look how it ended. You did need Rogue." She continued to stand there seething with righteous indignation.

"See, you didn't even think that I could handle one date without a service dog." Sam threw his arms in the air. "Don't worry, I won't be making that mistake again."

"What does that mean?" The anger fled and worry replace the emotion. Nelly sank back onto the couch.

"It means, miss dog trainer, that I won't be asking you out on another date. Not ever again. In fact, I won't ever ask another woman out. Tonight was proof that I'm not man enough to take a woman out for a nice meal, not even at a po-dunk diner." Sam turned his head and tried to cross his arms over his chest. But when he felt the holes in his arms through the long sleeve of his shirt, it only served to remind him of his shortcomings, and he put his hands down on the armrests of the chair.

Megan looked to Nelly and Jerod. "I think I need to talk to Sam alone. Nelly, if you want to talk about your brother, please call me and we can set up a time to meet."

All energy and fight left Nelly sitting there like a limp doll. Sam was breaking up with her before they were even a couple. Maybe it was for the best. She nodded and stood. When Jerod left the room, she followed and at the last minute looked back over her should at Sam, who had his face down.

*Chapter 28*

The next few days were filled with one-on-one sessions with Megan as well as daily group sessions with the rest of the men. But only in the evenings. Everyone, but Sam, still went over to Nelly's place to finish the clean out. At first, Sam thought he'd only take one or two days to himself, but when Megan agreed with him that he shouldn't go over there, he stayed back at the Crooked Arrow and worked on the ranch chores.

Every night at dinner, the men would talk about things they found in the house that day. At first, Sam didn't care. But by Thursday night, he began wishing he had the nerve to face Nelly. He wanted to be in on the adventures the men spoke about, but he also wanted to see Nelly. Which was stupid.

Sam knew he still cared for her, but also knew he was never going to be the man a woman like Nelly deserved.

On Friday morning, after Sam had finished the morning chores, Megan met him at the back door. "Sam, I think it's time you faced your fears and spoke with Nelly."

"Why? She's never going to forgive me for letting her brother commit suicide."

"Sam, how many times do we have to have this conversation? The actions of one man aren't your fault. You didn't bully him, and you didn't push him over the cliff. He made the decision to drive up to the top of the mountain and drive off. The note in his pocket was proof of his choice. Do you hear me? It was *his* choice." Megan put a hand on Sam's arm.

Sam looked up, expecting to see his counselor's warm, understanding eyes. But he was shocked to see the sternness there, instead. "But, if I had been at his side, I could have helped him."

Megan shook her head. "Which is it? If you had been with him you could have helped? Or, if you had died back in Afghanistan, you could have helped? What could you have done?"

Confusion and anger began to fill Sam's heart, and Rogue came over and nudged his leg. The dog had never left his side all week. And any time he began to spiral down, Rogue nudged him or whimpered to get his attention, and he was brought back to the present. He had to give it to Nelly, she was right. A service dog was exactly what he needed.

Then it hit him all of a sudden. "Nelly began to train service dogs for injured veterans right after Henry died, didn't she?"

Megan nodded and stayed quiet as she waited for Sam to think it all through.

"She felt guilty for his death, like me." Instead of waiting for Megan to agree with him, Sam walked away from her and continued to think out loud.

"She felt a need to help others like her brother the only way she knew how." He nodded to himself, then continued, "she once told me she felt the calling from God to train dogs for service members who suffered specifically from PTSD." He turned around and looked to Megan. "Like me."

Again, the counselor just nodded and waited for him to keep going.

"I could do this, too. Couldn't I?" This time, Sam stopped and waited for Megan to respond.

"Yes, if you wanted to work with service dogs, you could. Sam, you can do anything you put your mind to. Don't let your disability keep you from what you're feeling called to do." Megan had told him this same thing many times.

But it had never stuck, until now. "I can do all things through Christ which strengtheneth me. Philippians four thirteen." Sam had heard that verse repeated so many times, by so many different people over the years, that he had it memorized. But it had never hit his heart the way it did now. If he tapped into Christ's strength, he really could be a real man. Even with his missing arm. Sam paced away from Megan thinking hard about the possibilities. Then he turned around and smiled from ear to ear. "Do you think that I could work with Nelly, and her dogs?"

"I think anything is possible. But first, you have to apologize to her." Megan arched a brow.

She was right. Sam knew he'd been an absolute jerk. Actually, the word he used was one his aunt would have washed his mouth out for. So he kept

his words clean and thought about what he could
do to make it up to Nelly.

*Chapter 29*

T hank goodness for the dogs, and Megan. Even though Nelly wasn't a wounded vet, let alone a veteran, Megan had come by to see her a couple of times this week. Her mind was all over the place.

Sam had been her brother's best friend in the Army. They served side by side every day in a war zone. When Henry came home from the battle, he had surface wounds, sure, but it was his PTSD that got him a full medical discharge. Her brother had never told her about the horrors of war, just that it was tough. But she'd heard his nightmares at night, and seen the vacant expression turn to one of sheer agony at the strangest times.

And Sam had been through it all with Henry. In fact, Sam lost a limb. Something that time and a little medical attention couldn't really fix. While she had never thought a person who lost a limb was any less a human being, she knew some did think that way.

The fact that Sam lost most of his left arm serving his country didn't make him less, it made him more. In Nelly's eyes, he was a hero. A man who walked through a war zone and came out the other side stronger for it. Sure, Sam was still having difficulties adjusting to life and to what had happened to him, but he *was* adjusting. Nelly could see it.

Henry never did adjust. But her brother also didn't have the right support team. Even though Nelly hadn't served in the military, she had learned a lot from her brother in his letters and when he came home. Teamwork was what kept people alive in war. And without the proper team, most wouldn't survive. That was what basic training was all about. The military took a bunch of individuals, stiped their individual thought process, and turned them in a strong team. A team that could help each other survive the cruelest circumstances known to man.

Tears began to run down Nelly's face as she realized that had Henry been offered a spot in a place like the Crooked Arrow Ranch, he probably would be here with her today. And service dogs, like Rogue, were a huge part of the team that would help a veteran begin to recover. Nelly wasn't sure if a person would ever be the same after experiencing the atrocities of war, but she did believe with everything she had, that if a person had the right team, they could recover and grow into a better human being.

Spike nudged her leg, and Nelly smiled down at the dog who had stolen her heart. "Braver Hund." She scratched the area right above his eyes, and right between them. She knew that was the place Spike loved the most.

And of course, the other dogs couldn't be left out of loving attention, so they wagged their tales and tried to butt into the scratching and rubbing. Nelly laughed and her thoughts turned from her brother for a moment as she looked at each of her dogs. "Y'all are going to help your partners thrive, aren't you?"

Nelly got down on her knees and spread her arms wide. All three dogs came in for a group hug. After a few moments, the enthusiasm of the dogs and their need to be the closest to her, turned the game into dog pile. They all pushed her back, and then the dogs hovered over her licking her face and neck.

She was in that position, laughing and petting the dogs when a voice close by caught her attention. "Am I interrupting some sort of training?"

Immediately, Nelly felt the heat soar up her neck and into her face. The dogs, who must have heard the visitor enter, turned their attention from Nelly to him and wagged their tails as Sam walked over and began greeting each dog by name and petting their heads.

It gave Nelly a moment to collect herself and clean off the hay and dirt that was sure to be all over her body after rolling around on the barn ground with the dogs. "Sam, to what do we owe the pleasure?"

Nelly had hoped to see the man all week long, but when Megan told her that he was still dealing with the revelation, she understood his need to stay away. Even though it hurt. She dusted her hands against her jeans and shirt.

The look on Sam's face had her standing tall and feeling as though he was bringing bad news. He didn't wince, but his facial features tightened just enough to signal apprehension, or nervousness. She didn't know him well enough to know what each of his facial expression meant. Not yet at least.

He ran his right hand through his brown, slightly curly messed-up hair. It was a bit longer than he normally wore it, signifying he needed a cut. But she loved it longer. When he took off the cowboy hat he was wearing, Nelly figured he had been wringing his hands through his hair for a while. She almost asked him how long he sat outside in his truck before coming in.

"Am I still welcome here?" Sam put his hat back on his head and let both arms drop to his sides.

"Oh, of course you are." Nelly's heart ached for the man. "You'll always be welcome here, Sam."

He nodded. "Thank you. And I'm so sorry for the other night. I didn't handle things very well."

Nelly walked to him and put a hand on his right arm. "Sam, I get it. I haven't been through nearly as much as you have, and I was shocked, too. I can only imagine the memories that flooded through your mind." Her nose pricked and she hoped she wasn't about to cry, again. This past week she'd done enough crying.

Henry wouldn't want it.

But he *would* want her to befriend Sam. In fact, in one his letters he had even said she'd like him.

Sam took his hat off again and began turning it in his hands. "I was wondering if we could still be friends?"

She pulled him into a hug and felt her heart pitter-patter just as it always did when he was close. She also noticed his scent, it wasn't strong or overpowering. Oh boy, he had used her favorite cologne-Cool Water. Her nose picked up scents of mint, sandalwood, and something smokey. It mixed well with the earthy scent of the ranch. "Of course we can. Always."

When they pulled back, Nelly noticed his pupils were dilated. She hoped it meant he was still attracted to her. She knew he needed more time before they could actually start dating, he had more healing to do. But she hoped that when he was ready, he'd let her know.

Sam's Adam's apple bobbed a few times, then he cleared his throat. "I also have a favor to ask. Well, it's more than a favor."

"Come on, let's go get some tea and sit down. We can talk about whatever it is you'd like." Nelly led him to her little kitchenette where she had two camp chairs set up. "Please take a seat."

"How much longer before you can start living in the main house?" Sam hadn't been there at all that week, so he couldn't have known what all transpired.

"Well," Nelly put the kettle on and pulled out mugs and the tea bags. "I don't know how much any of the guys may have told you, but the house has been cleared of all junk."

"That's great. Congratulations, Nelly. So what's next?"

"The real work will begin. I'm going to have to replace quite a few walls. All of the flooring has to come up." Nelly winced and looked to Sam. "I think I'm also going to have to re-do most of the bathrooms."

"So, basically, you're going to gut the house and start over?" Sam shook his head and ran a hand down his face.

"Yeah. And it's gonna have to be very slow going. I don't have much money and I refuse to take out a loan on this place." Nelly looked around and quirked her lips to the side. "I can handle living in here for a while. At least until it starts to snow. Then, I'm not really sure."

"I can help," Sam blurted.

"Thank you, but as I said, I don't have much money. I couldn't offer you steady work." She tilted her head. "Do you have construction experience?"

A real smile, the kind that reached his eyes and lit them up like the night sky on a full moon. "I do. My dad is a general contractor and I grew up working with him during the summers and on other school breaks. I may not be able to do anything about plumbing or electrical, but I can take the walls down and put-up new drywall and paint them. I can do a lot of the labor myself. If you can buy the supplies, I would be willing to help for free."

Nelly shook her head adamantly. "No way. I can't let you work for free."

Sam stood and looked intently at Nelly. "How about a trade?"

She narrowed her eyes. "What sort of trade?" She didn't think he'd ask for anything untoward, but she had no idea what he would want in exchange for so much hard labor.

"It's nothing too hard. You train me on how to train service dogs. I want to help others like you and Rogue have helped me." Now, Sam didn't seem as confident as he did a moment ago.

"A certification course is required for you to open your own business. But, I can train you until you're ready to take the course." Actually, Nelly thought it would be a great idea. She could use the help with the house for sure, but he would have to apprentice with her for a few years if he wanted to be able to open his own business. And she could bring in more dogs and train more.

The sound of the tea kettle whistling brought her out of her thoughts and she jumped. "Oh, the tea."

Once they were both seated with their hot mugs of tea, she spoke, "Sam, are you serious about this? It's a major commitment. This is something that will take years before you can apply for your certification."

Sam thought for a moment, then set his mug down on the rickety table that sat between them. "Yes, I think it's a wonderful way of giving back for what I've been given. And I think Henry would really have liked us working together." A slight blush crept up his face and settled into his cheeks.

Nelly had wondered what all Henry told his battle buddy about her. He had spoken regularly about Sam, but not in personal details such as his full name. Had her brother tried to play matchmaker between them? Or did he just want them to be friends? Henry had spoken about he and Sam coming back to the states after their tour and starting a business together. They hadn't come up with a plan, but they did want to do something that would benefit veterans and military.

The more she thought about it, the more Nelly realized that her path had always been headed towards Sam. Even before she knew him.

# Chapter 30

The very next day Sam and Nelly had agreed to meet up for the Saturday pancake breakfast the Frenchtown Roasting Company. And it seemed most of the town was also in attendance. "Wow, was there some sort of memo sent out for the entire region to show up today?" Nelly chuckled when she met up with Sam, who had been standing in line. A line that looked at least thirty minutes, or more, long.

"Yeah, about that." Sam grinned. "Today is chocolate chip pancake day. Lottie does this once a month. It's a town favorite. Pretty much everyone comes and has their breakfast, or brunch, here."

"I guess that's one way to get the community together." Nelly looked down at Rogue and seeing he had his work vest on, kept herself from petting the dog. He sat their dutifully, only occasionally sniffing the air. She knew he'd be interested in the pancakes, but they weren't good for dogs.

"How are you and Rogue doing so far?" Nelly wanted to do some more work with the two, but she also knew that starting next week, Sam would be working with her at least twenty hours a week. And the rest of the time he'd be working on her house. The weeks where she didn't have enough money for supplies, he'd put more time in working with the dogs. So, she'd have plenty of time to get the two working together properly.

"He's been great. I can't tell you how glad I am that he chose me to be his partner. I never would have tried to get a service dog. Honestly, I didn't think I needed one. I thought they were for the blind or deaf, for the most part." Sam grinned down at Rogue. "Braver Hund. But I've come to learn that service dogs are so much more. They are true companions."

Rogue chuffed and nodded his head as though he agreed.

"I'm really glad you two bonded so well. I can't wait to see who bonds with one of my dogs next." Nelly had a few ideas, but she wouldn't share those thoughts with Sam. At least not while he was still a part of the Crooked Arrow Ranch. Those ideas were for Megan and Jerod. And she had a meeting with them later in the week to discuss exactly who she thought would pair well with each of her dogs.

"I'll be curious to see who Spike chooses." Sam laughed and it sent chills down Nelly's spine.

His laugh was so deep and joyful. He didn't laugh very often, but when he did, Nelly loved it. She prayed over time he'd laugh even more.

When they were finally seated and had received their pancakes, Nelly's eyes practically rolled to the back of her head. "Oh, wow. I had no idea chocolate and pancakes could be so wonderful."

She put a forkful of pancakes and pure maple syrup in her mouth again and moaned.

When she had swallowed her bite and opened her eyes, she noticed Sam staring at her lips. "What? Do I have syrup on my face?" She moved to wipe her chin just in case.

When she didn't get it, Sam smiled and rubbed his thumb along the side of her chin, and pulled it back. "See." He showed her the little bit of chocolate and then stuck the thumb in his mouth.

Nelly gasped. It was such an intimate act. Then she looked at his lips when he licked them. All thoughts of just being friends and waiting for him to be ready flew out the window. In that moment, she wanted nothing more than to pull him to her and kiss him like there was no tomorrow. Didn't matter that they were in the middle of the coffee shop with half the town surrounding them.

She leaned forward, still looking at his lips.

Sam leaned forward staring at her mouth.

They were in their own little bubble, not paying any attention to anyone around them. In fact, the noise had quieted and Nelly forgot they were in public. In her mind, it was just the two of them.

That was until a plate clanked on the table next to her, and she felt the brush of someone's shoulder sitting next to her.

"I'm not interrupting, anything? Am I?" Skeeter sat there grinning at them like the cat who caught the canary.

Nelly jerked back and blinked a few times as the roar of the Saturday crowd burst her bubble. "Skeeter. Good morning."

He winked at her then stuffed a giant forkful of chocolate chip pancake in his mouth and grinned as syrup oozed down the side of his mouth.

Nelly rolled her eyes and shook her head. The moment between her and Sam had been broken. But for just a moment, she thought he might have wanted to kiss her, too.

Then they were joined by Anthony and Mike from the ranch. All thoughts of a romantic breakfast were gone. Once they were all seated, Skeeter looked at the counter and asked, "who's that new girl?"

Nelly looked over to where Skeeter had pointed. "The blonde? That's Hope Lowry. She's Dana's cousin. Haven't you met her yet?"

Skeeter shook his head. "I think I'm in love."

"Don't let Jerod hear you say that. He's already set himself up as her big brother." Sam laughed and then finished the last bite of pancake on his plate.

Tony looked over his shoulder at the pretty girl and smiled.

Nelly caught the look between the two of them and realized that Skeeter was going to have some real competition for Hope's affections. The coming weeks would be a lot of fun if the way both men were smiling at Hope was any indication.

"Nelly, care to take a walk with me?" Sam stood and offered his hand.

While sitting around the table, talking and drinking coffee with the guys would have been fun, she also knew there was still a long line of people wanting to get inside for Lottie's special pancakes. "Yes, that'd be nice." She stood and took his hand.

As they walked outside, she realized that Sam had given her his left hand. The one that he always tried to keep away from everyone's attention. Nelly wondered if this meant he was finally comfortable enough with her to show her who he really was.

They walked in silence until they were away from the crowds around the coffee shop. Rogue was on duty and he had steered Sam away from one puddle, and from a group of guys who were a bit on the rowdy side. Nelly was proud of the dog for keeping an eye out.

Sam pulled them all down a side street where it was quieter and not so many tourists were congregating. "Nelly, I don't know if this is appropriate or not, but I'd like to try our date again. Would you be interested in having dinner with me Wednesday night?"

Sam looked her in her eyes when he asked her out. The confident man looking back at her made her nervous. Up until breakfast, she thought they were only going to be friends. But the way he had looked at her, and now the way held himself, she knew something major had changed for him, for the better.

"Yes, I'd like that." Nelly was going to like it very much, but she had to keep herself in check. While it did seem as though Sam had made some sort of breakthrough this week, she knew he had a long way to go before he was ready for a major commitment. And if she was honest with herself, she still had a few issues to deal with on her own.

When Wednesday rolled around, and Sam was at her barn door without Rogue, Nelly knew she was in trouble. He had on the Cool Water cologne again. And he wore black jeans, black boots, and a sky-blue button up cowboy shirt. A black cowboy hat was in his hands. Sam was the epitome of a sexy cowboy.

Nelly felt her cheeks flush and she was glad that she had chosen a pretty floral dress to wear for dinner that night. Sam had told her they were going to drive into Missoula for dinner. "You look...handsome." Her breathy voice startled her and she had to look away when she felt her cheeks warm.

"You, Nelly Wilson, take my breath away." Sam walked toward her and picked her hand up. When his lips lightly brushed her hand, she gasped.

In that very moment, Nelly knew she was a goner. This man had stolen her heart in a way that she never knew even existed. He was so different from the men she'd dated in the past. Her resolve to take things slowly was beginning to crack.

"Are you ready?" Sam took her hand and put it in the crook of his arm and led her to his truck.

At dinner, conversation flowed so easily. They even spent a little bit of time talking about Henry. And for the first time since his death, Nelly didn't cry when she thought of him.

"I think your brother would approve." Sam had her hand in his as they walked down the street, looking at the shop windows along the avenue.

"So do I." She squeezed his hand and realized that if Henry were still alive, he would have brought them together the moment Sam was out of the hospital.

"You know, one night when it was really cold out. Henry had received a letter from you with a bag of cookies." Sam chuckled and looked up into the sky. "We sat there on his bunk talking about you and he told me that he wanted us to meet."

"Really? He told me I'd like you when we met." Nelly thought back to her letter from Henry and wondered if it was after this night of the two sharing her homemade chocolate chip cookies.

"We both wondered why you always included a slice of bread with the cookies." Sam looked to her and quirked a brow. "Was there some special meaning?"

Joy filled her heart and when her nose began to twitch, she knew that if she shed any tears now, they would be tears of joy and happy memories. "When cookies have to be shipped, I always put a slice of bread in the bag. It keeps them fresher, longer."

"So, that's why Henry's cookies were always the best. The rest of us just thought you had some special recipe. I even asked him once to get your recipe from you. When he told me that you used the one on the bag of chocolate chips, I didn't believe him. I thought he wanted to keep the secret recipe in the family, or something." Sam laughed and looked back up at the stars. "Do you think he's looking down on us right now and smiling?"

"I do." Nelly looked up and watched the stars begin their nightly trek across the sky. She sent up a silent prayer thanking God for putting her on Sam's team, and for being the head of their team.

"Nelly?"

"Yes." She pulled her gaze from the sky and looked to Sam. His face was so close to hers. When he inched even closer, her heart picked up speed and her stomach began doing somersaults. She prayed he would kiss her.

Sam stayed quiet and he slowly inched closer to her. His gaze moved from her eyes to her lips and then back again.

In one sense, it felt like ages before his lips met hers, but in another, it felt like it came too fast. His lips were warm and soft. The kiss was sweet, not the least bit demanding.

Sam wrapped his arms around her back. Nelly put one arm on his chest where she felt his heart beating just as wildly as hers. Her other hand grabbed the side of his shirt and held on tight.

When he opened his lips, she reciprocated. A heady sense filled her head and she never wanted it to end. Before the kiss went very long, a car drove by and honked. Someone yelled out, "get a room." Then they honked again.

Both of them pulled back and Nelly giggled.

Sam put his right hand on her face and looked her in the eyes. "I want this, I do. But you should know I need to take it slow. Like super slow."

Her nose began to prick and she hoped she didn't start to cry. This man was so warm and sweet. He was exactly what she needed and wanted. "I think slow is good."

Sam leaned forward and kissed the tip of her nose.

"Then, I think I should get you home before it's too late." He led them back to his truck and to toward their new beginning. A beginning that both knew had been orchestrated by God, and helped along by Henry before either of them ever realized.

So, what did you think? I hope and pray that I did a good job representing what a wounded soldier goes through when he, or she, comes home. While I did serve in the US Army, I never saw war. Unfortunately, I have experienced the horrors of a military doctor who didn't care, and a VA system that wasn't geared toward treating the wounded.

While I served, I hurt my back. It would have been fine if I'd had received proper medical treatment, but back then, when a young soldier complained of back pain, they usually ignored us. However, the past ten years has seen a dramatic improvement of pain management and overall treatment in the VA system. I have to say, that my VA doctors have partnered with some of the best specialty care doctors in the US. I know that the treatment of vets is improving, but there is still a long road to go for those who suffer from PTSD.

While that wasn't something I had to deal with, I know too many returning heroes who do have had to deal with it, and they don't always get the treatment they need. The military is changing, but they still don't do the best at recognizing the symptoms, and then treating the person properly.

Only recently has the VA begun to use service dogs, and not just companion dogs, to help a veteran get control of their PTSD. The dogs still aren't widely used, but more and more studies are coming back to show the benefits of service animals on mental illness. I hope you'll join me in praying for our heroes and their recovery.

If you know of someone who is suffering from PTSD, or any mental illness, there is hope. There is help. The greatest doctor we can have is the Lord. And He does use doctors here on Earth to help Him in His treatment of patients. Please, reach out to the VA crisis line, or your local suicide prevention line, if someone is thinking of harming themselves. Every day there are new resources available.

While the Crooked Arrow Ranch was a made-up ranch, there are services out there like what Jerod and his team are offering. Check with Wounded Warriors Project, or others like it, to find groups outside the VA that can help.

This is just the first book in the series, so keep an eye out for more coming in the Crooked Arrow Ranch series. Join my newsletter and get the free story of how Jerod met Dana. And if you enjoy Christmas reads, then check out my Big Sky Christmas series to read more about Frenchtown, Montana, and the Frenchtown Roasting Company. There's also quite a few of the guys from the Crooked Arrow in books 3-4 of the Big Sky Christmas series.

And please, pray for your wounded veterans, even if you are reading this in another country. Anyone who serves their country with honor deserves to be honored by the citizens of their country.

And as a little side note, putting a slice of bread into a Ziplock baggie when you store cookies does help to keep them moist, longer. My grandmother used to send me her homemade cookies in a Ziplock baggie with one slice of bread. The cookies weren't always whole, but even the little pieces were moist and tasty! I always loved getting a care package from my grandma.

May God bless you all and keep you safe in the new year!

*And keep reading until the end to see the next book in this wonderful and rich new series!

# Contact Me

For those of you who love social media, here are the various ways to follow or contact me:

BookBub: https://www.bookbub.com/authors/jenna-hendricks

Instagram: https://www.instagram.com/j.l.hendricks/

Twitter: https://twitter.com/TinkFan25

Facebook: https://www.facebook.com/people/JL-Hendricks/100011419945971

Website: https://jennahendricks.com

# Free Short Story

F ree short story when you join my newsletter
See how Jerod and Dana met and fell in love today!
https://jennahendricks.com/newsletter/

**Wounded Hearts Ranch**

By Jenna Hendricks

Jerod's war wounds are more than skin deep. Will he allow Dana to get close enough to heal his wounded heart?

# *Sneak Peek at the next book*

Hope's Healing Love is book 2 in the Crooked Arrow Ranch series, and it's available for pre-order now. It will go live on February 15. But if you pre-order it now, it'll be downloaded to your account as soon as it's live!

**It'll take more than fireworks to scare this cowgirl away.**

Anthony Sullivan grew up on a ranch, so when he was given the chance to recuperate at the Crooked Arrow Ranch, he knew that was the right place for him.

Dana Baker's cousin, Hope Lowry, moved to Frenchtown, Montana to help her aunt and uncle run their ranch. *She didn't come to town to meet a handsome wounded veteran.* No siree, no way. Ahhh, chicken and hash! Why can't a girl get a break from handsome men?

**But Anthony isn't interested in a romance. He needs Hope's help to get the Crooked Arrow**

ranch up to snuff.

*When the 4th of July parade causes more sparks than a whole crate of sparklers, what's a girl to do? Will Anthony be able to handle the explosions in the sky as well as those in his heart?*

**And what's going on at the Crooked Arrow ranch that has Anthony worried about its future?**

Be sure to come back to Frenchtown, Montana, and meet the newest couple! Plus, see which dog will end up taking center stage in this new wounded veteran clean romance.

Hope's Healing Love

https://www.amazon.com/gp/product/B09P5MX 551

www.ingramcontent.com/pod-product-compliance
Lightning Source LLC
Chambersburg PA
CBHW010841190726
48286CB00012BA/2939